THE HOUSE THAT LOU BUILT

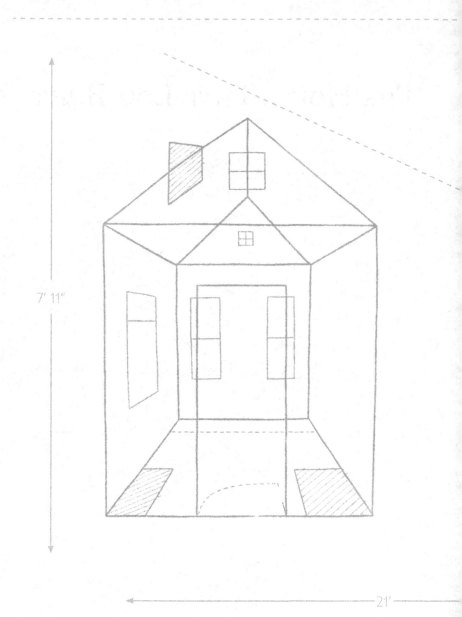

7' 11"

21'

The House
That Lou Built

Mae Respicio

THORNDIKE PRESS
A part of Gale, a Cengage Company

Farmington Hills, Mich • San Francisco • New York • Waterville, Maine
Meriden, Conn • Mason, Ohio • Chicago

LIBRARY OF CONGRESS CIP DATA ON FILE.
CATALOGUING IN PUBLICATION FOR THIS BOOK
IS AVAILABLE FROM THE LIBRARY OF CONGRESS

ISBN-13: 978-1-4328-6593-1 (hardcover alk. paper)

Published in 2019 by arrangement with Random House Children's Books, a division of Penguin Random House LLC

Printed in Mexico
1 2 3 4 5 6 7 23 22 21 20 19

To my mom,
Tina Respicio

CHAPTER 1
IF PEOPLE WERE HOUSES

If people were houses, Lola Celina, my grandmother, would be a hot-pink Painted Lady — one of those fancy San Francisco Victorians tourists love, with intricate stained glass that casts rainbows onto the sidewalks. She's colorful. Right now, we're strutting around the living room in summery folk-dance dresses. Mine's bright yellow. It feels light and airy, and when I'm jumping around in it I wish I could fly.

I spin as fast as I can. The skirt flounces up and Lola joins me, twirling and twirling, while Mom takes our picture from the couch. We finish and stand shoulder to shoulder, trying not to wobble. Laughter pours out of us.

"Ay nako!" Lola says. "I haven't danced around this much since I was —"

"— crowned Miss Sampaguita in your village for three years in a row, we all know," Mom says, and Lola cracks up. My cousins and I have heard this story a million times; it's one of my favorites.

Lola and I put our arms around each other. I'm taller than she is now. I'm only half Filipina, so we don't look exactly alike, but our family says we have the same smile. Definitely the same crazy laugh.

I plop down next to Mom, out of breath.

"Lou, we should get you a pretty dress to wear on your birthday," Mom says.

"Actually, what I think every new thirteen-year-old needs is a circular saw," I say, even though she'd never go for that. Too dangerous.

"Nice try, kiddo."

"Don't you want to wear something

beautiful on your special day, *anak ko*?" Lola says. *Anak ko.* My child. Even though she calls all the grandkids that, it still makes me feel special.

My birthday's coming up, but I don't care about wearing some silly dress or having a huge Sweet Thirteen like some of the kids at school. There's only one thing I want — my own house.

I just have to build it first.

The idea started off as a daydream, a dare to myself: What if I made something no other girl has? Because here's the neat part: I own some land. Trees and shrubs and everything. I inherited it from my dad's family after he died, and that's where my house will go.

I've been planning this for a while, and I'm ready to do something about it. If I keep thinking and brainstorming and watching how-to videos — instead of *doing* — it's never going to happen. Lolo, my grandfather, used to say, "That's how dreams work. You just have to do them."

"Okay, scooch over," Lola says, sitting next to us. She starts folding and piling up costumes she sewed for Barrio Fiesta.

Barrio Fiesta is a neighborhood celebration. Villages in the Philippines throw them every year. It's our big fund-raiser for the Filipino American Community Senior Center, with dizzying rides, tasty food, and all my friends hanging out. The festival ends in a show, and my whole family pitches in. This time Lola's sewing, I'm making sets, and Mom's organizing the rummage sale. I'm dancing, too. We only practice a couple days a week, so that leaves me plenty of building time.

Mom tilts her head against mine. She's quiet.

"What's wrong, my dear Minda? Is this about your job search?" Lola asks.

"I haven't gotten any offers yet. I applied all over the area," Mom says.

"It's okay, *anak*. Try to be patient. And you should feel proud, too. It's not easy to put yourself through school. It's all right to take things slow."

My mom's a medical technician, but she just got her nursing degree by going to school at night. Now she's looking for a new job as a nurse, and works a lot of overtime to pay off student loans — and because we're saving up to move out of

Lola's house.

Mom's face brightens a little. "The good news is the hospital I interviewed with in Washington State scheduled a follow-up call. Cross your fingers."

Is she serious? I sit up. "Are you talking about moving?"

Mom smooths my hair. "I've been thinking a lot about it, honey, and it's the perfect time for a change."

"Not that kind of change." I can't imagine anything worse.

"San Francisco's so expensive. If we lived in Washington, we could find our own place and save up for your college fund." She smiles at me like she hasn't just said the wrong thing.

I give her a big smile back. "We're. Not. Moving."

Lola rubs small circles onto Mom's shoulders, the way she and Mom do with me whenever I'm feeling bad. "You'll find a job soon, *anak ko.* Though I cannot imagine you and Lou moving so far from home."

"Well, something good will come our way, I know it," Mom says. She turns to me. "Okay, young lady, if you're done parading around like Miss Preteen Sampaguita, then it's bedtime. Last day of seventh grade tomorrow!"

I lie in bed, staring at glow-in-the-dark stars on the ceiling. I wish I was looking at real stars on my land, where at night they fill the sky. The thought of moving has me wide-awake. I can't believe Mom would want a job in another state.

Most people count sheep to fall asleep. Me? I like to think about houses. It cheers me up. And it's easy, because there are hundreds of types of houses in the world.

Some I like just for their names: the barndominium, the geodesic dome, and the Queenslander; a saltbox, a snout house, or a Yaodong.

Others have fascinating details, like:

The yurt — a round, portable tent pulled in carts by yaks.

The houseboat — part house and part boat.

The mansion — everybody knows this one. It's what I used to want to live in, but now I think they're obnoxious, too big and glossy. Not my style.

Then there's the opposite: a tiny house.

These houses are garage-sized small, but they can still have a kitchen and a bathroom and a secret cranny for brainstorming ideas.

People all around the world build and live in them. They don't cost as much as a normal house and certainly not as much as a mansion. But the best part? A tiny house fits everything anyone could ever need — a bed, a table and chairs, a toilet, a sink with running water (which a lot of people in the world don't even have). If you think of it that way, a tiny house isn't tiny at all. It's just right.

Mom snores loudly from her side of our room while cars zoom down the street. We live in a busy part of the neighborhood where shops and restaurants and gas stations stay open way late. Sometimes I can trick myself into thinking traffic sounds like the ocean.

Mom and I share a bedroom, with twin beds shoved up against opposite walls. It's the same room she shared with her sister, my auntie Gemma, growing up.

Lolo, my grandfather Ernesto, died a few years ago, but I still see him in every part of this place: On the patio where he and I would watch sunsets like movies, a wad of tobacco in Lolo's cheek. In the kitchen where he fed me rice and fish, *kamayan* style — with his hands, no utensils. He said it made the food taste better. It did. And in this very room, at night, tucking me in.

He'd pull the blanket to my chin, and I'd run my fingers down his gnarled knuckles and listen to stories about his job when he first came to America. He picked crops in fields, his back aching, a straw hat full of holes the only thing shielding him from the sun. After stories he'd close my door, but I could still hear Lola in the kitchen washing dishes, even though there's a dishwasher. She'd say, "I never needed a dishwasher in the Philippines, did I?"

Now it's just me, Mom, and Lola. Lolo died three years ago, but we first moved in when I was a little kid. Mom had me when she was only nineteen, a kid herself. At least, that's how our family gossips

14

about it. And now here we are, Mom snoring like a chain saw.

Having my own room would be awesome-sauce.

"Mom?" I whisper. No answer. She's out.

From under the bed I slip out a flashlight and a long, fat cylinder of paper. My blueprint.

It crinkles as I pull off the rubber band and roll the paper open like a giant map. It's soft and thin under my fingers, full of notes and numbers. I shine the light.

The land I own belonged to Dad's family, the Nelsons — my dad, Michael Nelson; Grandpa Ted; and Grandma Beverly. Dad died in a car accident a month before I was born, so we never met. But I have his land, so at least I know some part of him.

I wasn't going to start construction until I had all the materials, but if Mom wants to move us away, I might never have the chance to build. Once she has an idea, that's all she can focus on. Me too. Stubbornness is one of the traits Lola says Mom and I share.

My shop teacher, Mr. Keller, has a quote up in his classroom that I like: *Seize the day.* That's what I'll do.

"Lucinda, go to sleep." Mom glances my way before turning over, her back to me like a wall.

I shut off the flashlight and bury myself under the covers. When it seems like she's asleep, I aim a bright circle onto my plans.

My new house will have a composting toilet and, right above the kitchen, a cozy sleeping loft. Giant picture windows will frame redwoods. Anytime I need to get away for peace and quiet, I'll go there.

Time to make it real. Seize the day!

CHAPTER 2
THE HOUSE I'M
GOING TO BUILD

Whenever Mr. Keller sees people goofing off during shop, he points at them with his nub and says, "Careful or you'll lose a digit." His finger ends at the joint. He lost the tip in high school while not paying attention during shop. Everyone gets freaked when they see the stub up close — including me. Right now it's hovering a few inches from my face, pale and smooth around the bone. I try not to look.

"Miss Bulosan-Nelson?" he shouts.

"Sorry," I say.

"No staring off into space, please."

Jack Allen glances over and I'm sure he's smirking, but whatever. It's the last day of school and I can finally start building something big.

Mr. Keller looks about a thousand years old. Mom says when she had him in high school, he already looked ancient.

He's mainly bald, with a half circle of gray hair rimming his head and long white whiskers that poke out from different parts of his cheeks. He likes to pluck them while reminding us of how we're the only public middle school in San Francisco that offers woodworking (aka Industrial Arts and Technology) and how that's good since electronic doo-zads have made the human race manually incompetent. Kids take his class because they think they can breeze through, until they find out just how hard it is to make a wooden banana hanger.

"Power off any tools, folks. It's your last Keller's Critique!" he shouts.

The buzzing in the room dies down as everyone waits for the machinery to come to a complete stop. If there's anything Mr. K has taught us, it's the importance of safety.

I slide off my goggles as he circles the tables.

Someone's working on an "electronics holder" — basically a hunk of wood to stick a phone on top of (genius). Some other guy's making what he calls "Mystery in a Cube" — yet another shapeless block. Then there's my piece.

Mr. Keller puts his hands on his knees to get eye level with it. He pushes his glasses up and stares into the model of a teeny-tiny house.

"May I?" he asks, and I nod.

He picks it up carefully. It's small enough to fit into his cupped palms, with four walls, an A-frame roof, card-sized cutouts for windows, and a door. I didn't have time for the deck.

"Is this for birds? Some kind of wonderful, magical birdhouse?" he asks, perking up. He always seems genuinely curious about what I make.

"No."

"Then what is it?" He knocks on the

roof like some mini-creature might pop out to say hi.

The room's quiet, everyone's listening, waiting for a new Tissue Rejuvenator moment. That was my fifth-grade Innovation Project, a toilet-paper-dispenser hat so that whenever I had a cold I could reach up, yank down the paper, and *presto*! Instant relief! I was so nervous during the presentation, but everyone cheered and they all wanted to try it on. I love it when people get excited about things I make.

But as I sat down again, Jack Allen laughed, leaned over, and whispered, "Nice work, TP Girl. . . ." Meathead Carver Jamison heard and shouted, "Lou the Toilet Paper Girl for president! She gives free wipes!" Everyone busted up. They still call me President TP.

I haven't told many kids at school about my house, but this is the most excited I've felt about any of my ideas — and I've had a lot.

Mr. Keller hands my project back.

"It's a model for the house I'm going to build." I sound confident. I say it louder so everyone can hear: "I'm building my own house."

"Your own birdhouse?" Mr. Keller asks.

Maybe I should talk them through my vision, like the floorboards I'll fit together from reclaimed hardwood, or the twinkle lights I'll drape over the deck in a sparkly canopy. All this in one hundred square feet, the size of some people's luxury bathrooms.

I look around, but no one's paying attention. "Yeah. A birdhouse." It's easier than explaining.

Mystery in a Cube Guy snickers. "Who makes *birdhouses*?"

"Who makes a square?" I shoot back.

"Enough," Mr. Keller snaps.

Jack peers my way again and, when I catch him, he looks down at the thing he built — bookends, I think? Simple blocks, barely sanded. I bet they're not even level.

Mr. Keller runs his good hand along the seams of my model like he's checking for gaps. "Excellent detailing, Lucinda." He says this quietly so that no one else can hear. He's a nice teacher like that.

The bell rings for lunch period. Mr.

Keller gives a few parting words and the class transforms into a flurry of cleanup.

Once the room clears, I say, "Mr. K, you have a sec?"

"Of course. Anything for my hardest-working student." He sits down at his desk.

"What would you think if I was building my own house?"

"Let's see. I would probably think it was a huge undertaking, but one that I would certainly delight in seeing you accomplish. I certainly *wood.* Get it? *Would?*" he says, chortling. I let that one go.

"It's called a tiny house."

"That's a beguiling concept," he says. "I've read about them."

I want to ask Mr. Keller for tips, like, well, how do I know if I'm starting the right way? Or even if he'll help me bring a few things to my land. He's always bragging about the new truck he just bought.

"I have some stuff I need hauled to my building site, and I'm trying to find help.

It shouldn't take too long," I say.

"Perhaps I could be of assistance," he says cheerily. I knew he'd volunteer.

"Really? That'd be great."

"Sure, I know a guy. He'll cut you a deal. I'll call your mother and give her the info. It'll be a good excuse for us to catch up."

Mr. Keller goes way back with my family. He and Lolo first met while playing chess at Golden Gate Park, around the time Mr. K still had hair. Mom and Auntie Gemma had him for social studies and homeroom in high school, and Lola often invites him and his husband to our parties.

He opens his lunch container and makes a sour face. "Organic avocado and dry alfalfa sprouts. Ed's trying to kill me." He extends half his sandwich. "Care to join? We'll talk more about this wee house of yours."

"Thanks, maybe another time." I grab my things and head out to meet Alexa and Gracie.

We eat lunch at our normal hilltop spot, on a bench with my favorite view of steep streets that dip like roller coasters.

Gracie's Filipina, too, and the nicest girl in our grade. We take folk dance together and our families are close. Alexa became my friend in kindergarten when Carver Jamison threw sand at me and she made him cry by dumping a pail of sand on his head. Alexa gets a lot of *hey*s in the hallway. She's friendly and never snooty, so everyone likes her.

I'm not as popular as my friends. People say I'm kind of quiet — except when it comes to my ideas. When I create something, I want everyone to know.

Lola says that "quiet" means I notice everything, and it's what I had in common with both of my grandpas. She says I spot things that need fixing and think up ways to fix them, the type of person who needs to work with her hands.

I squeeze in on the bench.

"Hi, Ate," Gracie says.

"Hi, Manang," Alexa says.

It makes me laugh whenever Alexa calls me Manang. Even though Alexa's blond and blue-eyed, she's an honorary Filipina. She's been around our families long enough to know that if you see someone who's Filipino, even if they're not related, you should call them by their respectful term.

My family uses *manang* or *manong* for older siblings and cousins, and *ading* for younger ones — in Gracie's family they use *kuya* for brothers and *ate* for sisters. Our words are different because the Philippines has so many dialects.

We pull out our lunches.

"Ew, what's that stuff all over your hair?" Alexa asks, and their faces pinch up.

Gracie blows at the top of my head. Sawdust.

"Woodshop," I say.

"Louie, maybe next year you should try a cooler elective, ooh, like Peer Mediation. Or, I know, High-Velocity Dance! You'd be great," Gracie says.

"And anyway, the only cute guy in shop is Jack Allen." Alexa smiles slyly as he walks past. "Speaking of Jack . . ."

All the girls watch him like that. They gossip like he's famous or something. Jack's a surfer-guy who's always in shorts and flip-flops. He has darkish tan skin and longish dark hair that's not styled with goop like some of the other boys'. He has lots of different kinds of friends at school, a floater.

Jack breezes past with a super-cool group, the kids who make middle school look easy and fun. I catch the gaze of one of the girls, someone pretty in a teen-magazine kind of way.

"What's up, Prez TP?" she says, giggling. Alexa and Gracie roll their eyes.

I expect Jack to laugh but he says, "Hey, Lou." He looks straight at me, and not in a you're-a-weird-DIY-girl kind of way. Friendly. He probably thinks he can still get help with his woodblocks so he won't flunk our last assignment. I'm too shy to say anything back, and he keeps walking. Gracie and Alexa glance at each other.

"What?" I say.

"He's never said hey to you before . . . ,"

Gracie says.

". . . out loud . . . and in public!" Alexa says.

They give me huge smiles and I blush. I dig into my lunch bag and pull out a plastic container that I don't remember packing. Inside, there's rice and little dried fish with the heads still on. I call them Salty Snackers, but only at home.

"You gotta tell Lola to stop packing your lunch. No one brings that to school, not even the Asian kids. Ask for bologna next time," Gracie says.

Alexa plucks out a tiny fishy, swims it in front of Gracie's face, and pops it into her mouth. "Mmmmm . . . tasty."

I've asked Lola to stop, but she always sneaks things in.

"Almost weekend time," Alexa says. She bites into the sunflower seed butter sandwich her mom packs every Friday — on sprouted whole grain with the crusts cut off. There are hearts and clouds and smiley faces drawn on the plastic bag.

"You guys have plans?" I ask.

"It's Ultimate Saturday to kick off summer vacay," Gracie says, grinning.

Ultimate Saturday is when Gracie and her dad do something special, just the two of them, like gourmet cooking classes or trapeze school.

"Nice. What are you guys doing this time?" Alexa asks.

"We're renting those bright yellow go-carts tourists drive down Lombard Street." She gives me two thumbs up and laughs.

"My dad and I did that once. You're gonna have sooooo much fun!" Alexa says. "I'm hiking with my dad. He found a waterfall in Marin that we've never been to. You should come with us, Lou."

My friends love to talk about the cool dad things they do. They always invite me, but I make up excuses not to go. Since I'm dad-less, I think they feel bad and don't want to leave me out. I'm lucky we try to take care of each other that way.

If Mom and I have to move, how will I ever find friends like them again? I stop eating.

"Gotta go help with eighth-grade promotional," Gracie says, getting up. "See you at fiesta practice, Lou."

"Okay," I say.

Alexa looks at me. "So you want to go hiking with us?"

"Thanks, I can't." I've got my house to build.

"How about dinner later?"

That I would love. Alexa's family always eats dishes we never have at home, and her parents talk to us like we're not little kids. I'm fascinated by how normal her life seems. It's like a science experiment to me. It has a mom and a dad who are still married and a big brother who comes home from college on weekends; a perfect nucleus enclosed in a red-and-cream Spanish Colonial Revival with a hybrid car tucked into the garage. My normal? A gigantic extended family squished into Lola's for every holiday imaginable.

Alexa waves her hands at my face like I've forgotten about her. I do that sometimes, get stuck in my head even with people right in front of me.

"Hello?" she says. "My house later? It's

Vegan Lasagna Night!"

"Sure." I smile at her. "I'll ask my mom."

We look out at our view of clouds framing the sky and houses packed on roads that slope into each other. I can't wait for this day to end. Once summer break starts, so will my house.

CHAPTER 3
PERFECT HOME

I gather with my Barrio Fiesta crew on-stage in the senior center auditorium. We've had a long Friday afternoon of dance practice and set-building as we finish up the *bahay kubo,* a little home. We've made the walls out of huge sheets of cardboard and painted on the bamboo patterns. Now it needs the roof.

A group of girls glue straw pieces onto the house while the boys chase each other with unplugged hot-glue guns.

Every Barrio Fiesta ends in a spectacular show by the kids. This year's skit tells the story of a boy in the Philippines whose *bahay kubo* gets caught in a flood, but the neighbors help his family escape by carrying the house to safety.

A *bahay kubo* is the first type of house I ever learned of, because Lola used to sing us songs about them. It's the traditional Philippine house, built on stilts, with one room where the whole family lives. At night they unroll a mat and everyone sleeps on it, and in the morning they just roll it up again before getting on with their day. If the land floods during typhoons, villagers help their neighbors by hoisting the house onto their shoulders with wooden poles and walking it to its next spot.

This ancient tradition has a name: *Bayanihan.* Community. Helping each other. We chose it as this year's festival theme.

Right now the boys aren't helping at all.

Arwin, my second cousin, runs after Cody, another half-Filipino kid like me. Cody's my dance partner. Arwin chases Cody to our work area, and loose straw flies. The boys drop to the floor, laughing and out of breath.

"Hey, the house looks really good," Arwin says, surprised. "We did a nice job."

"We?" I say. The boys barely did anything.

"Lou, when are you going to start building your house?" Gracie asks.

"Stay tuned," I say, smiling at her.

"Girls don't build houses — they only *vacuum* them." Cody cracks up.

"Lame," Gracie says.

"FYI, women build and invent lots of things. A woman invented the circular saw in the eighteen hundreds," I say.

Gracie sticks her finger on Cody and makes a sizzle noise. "Burn!"

"Big whoop," says Gordon. Gordon's a half-Chinese, half-Filipino kid whose hair looks like someone stuck a bowl on his head and cut right around it.

"Oh yeah, and inventors of the life raft, the bulletproof vest, *and* residential solar heating? Women," I say.

Gracie and I high-five. I've memorized a long list of female inventors. My name will be on it one day.

"Lou's not bad at making stuff. Better than you jerks," Arwin says. He points the glue gun at the boys and chases them off.

Gracie and another girl hoist up the house, and I stand back to check out our hard work. "Nice!" Everyone's going to ooh and aah once they see it dramatically lit up with spotlights.

My family's had fun at this festival ever since I was little. Lolo used to sneak goodies to me from all the food booths, and my cousin Sheryl and I would sink down into the theater seats to watch her big sister, Maribel, swirl onstage. The music always went on past dark — sometimes I wouldn't remember going to sleep, I'd just wake up the next morning in bed, still in my folk-dance costume. If Mom and I move, I'll miss all this. I'd hate that for sure.

Sheryl and her mom, Auntie Gemma, wave as they walk up. Auntie's holding a bag of skirt sashes for Lola to fix. Arwin yanks one out and flicks it at Sheryl. She grabs another, and they start flicking each other.

Manang Sheryl is my best friend and

my cousin. She loves the festival but *hates* the dancing part. She gets nervous — like, about-to-faint nervous — but Auntie still makes her perform.

Sheryl's already thirteen and has taught me everything Mom hasn't, like what happens when you French kiss (gross) and why I should wear "cute" things like skirts. She hasn't given up on me yet, even though I'm sticking with jeans and Converse (way comfier).

Sheryl's full Filipina and looks more like my mom than I do, with tan skin and black hair trailing down her back, swingy like in a shampoo commercial. She's short with a sporty build and already wears a real bra — she's not pancake-flat like I am.

"Great work, girls!" Auntie says.

It's not too shabby, but I can usually find things to fix.

"It still needs more straw at the top! Everybody grab some and help," I say, but Auntie pulls on my arm.

She says, "Come on, gang. Time to go."

When we walk into Lola's, we see Arwin's older brother, Manong Kelvin, sitting at the dining table, shoveling Lola's famous stewed okra into his mouth and reading a textbook.

"What's going on, Kelvin?" Auntie says. Kelvin goes to college close by and visits between classes to eat or nap or wash his clothes.

Without glancing up, he mumbles, like it's one word, "HiAuntieLaundry."

Sheryl and Arwin pat his full cheeks, puffed with rice and stew. He shoos them away.

Lola's house has family pictures covering every wall. I always think the faces are creepily staring at me. Souvenirs, like Las Vegas snow globes, cram the shelves, and plastic shields everything — the carpet, the lamps, even the TV. It's small, but we can squeeze in a ton of people.

My family's close. Literally. Sheryl and Maribel live only four blocks away, and everyone else drops in whenever they want — they can't leave each other alone. Lola says that as the eldest of fourteen siblings, it's her job to take care of everyone. That would drive me nuts.

"Who's ready for dinner?" Mom asks

from the kitchen.

"We're just dropping off more costumes for Lola to hem." Auntie sets the bag down. "What are you cooking? Smells yummy."

"Lola made chocolate meat," Mom says. That's code for *dinuguan,* a tasty pork dish cooked in pork blood. Normally I love Filipino food, but today I'm tired of it.

"May I go to Alexa's for dinner? Her mom's making lasagna," I say, even though Sheryl's listening. She hates not getting invited to things.

"The rubber-cheese kind you don't like?" Mom says.

"Should I ask Alexa if you can come?" I say to Sheryl, but she shakes her head.

"It's okay."

Sheryl and Arwin settle in and scoop rice onto their plates. Kelvin dumps his bowl into the sink and shouts, "Thanks, Lola! Thanks, Aunties!" He slings on his backpack, straps on a helmet, and jets out the door. This house fills up and empties out without warning, so I never know when I might have quiet time.

"Please?" I say. "It's basically summer break now."

Mom smiles at me. "Let me just call over there to make sure it's okay."

At Alexa's house I ring the bell and her mom greets me with a big hug. She's a tall, slender woman with light hair and dark roots, and she always makes me feel welcome.

"Lou, the official eighth grader! How's it feel? Come on in, I'll grab Lexy for ya," she says as she walks up the stairs.

I love Alexa's place, with all its happy colors and books and weird abstract art. It's sunshiny and cheerful, just like her family. If my friend were a house, she'd definitely be this one.

Alexa runs down the stairs and ambushes me with a giant hug, too.

"Can you girls set the table, please? Dinner in a few minutes."

"Yes, sir. Right away, sir." Alexa gives her mom a stiff salute.

We begin setting the table while some sort of rumba music plays, the kind Lola and the aunties would start dancing to if they heard it.

I'm still thinking about Mom wanting to leave San Francisco. I lay down a place mat and Alexa tops it with a plate.

"Question. What would happen if I weren't around anymore?" I ask.

Alexa gives me the strangest look. She plunks down the entire stack of plates and her eyes get wide. "Oh my gosh, Louie . . . Are you . . . dying?"

I laugh. "No, silly. I mean like if I moved or something."

"Phew!" she says. "But wait. . . . You better not say that you're moving. I would hate you forever."

"We're not. At least, I don't think so."

"Then why are you flipping out?"

"My mom said she's looking at a nursing job in a whole different *state.* Washington."

"But we're supposed to go to high school together, then do our gap year in Paris before we go to New York for college, remember?"

"Right? Am I overreacting?"

"No! But don't worry about it, Louie.

Dessert will make you feel better. Mom whipped up some dairy-free wheatgrass ice cream with dehydrated kiwis. That should get your mind off things," she says, making a face, and we laugh.

Alexa, her dad, and I sit around the table, and her mom sets down the star dish. They clap, so I join them.

Dinner here looks different from meals at my family's, especially lately, since Mom's always working double shifts. When that happens, Lola and I eat on TV trays while watching design shows. Alexa's mom forces them to sit down together every night, and even though Alexa complains about it, I think it's neat.

"Dig right in, ladies!" her dad says.

Alexa's parents sip from the same wineglass and tuck into their lasagna.

"So, Lou, Lexy tells us you want to build your own little house?" her dad says. Normally he's in a suit, but tonight he's got on his red Stanford sweatshirt.

"I've seen some of those on TV," Alexa's mom says. "I always wonder what it would be like to live in one."

"I don't know anyone who'd be able to do that but Louie," Alexa says.

They're all smiling at me.

The first person I ever told I wanted to build a house was my mom. She looked surprised and asked, "Why?"

"Because Dad was going to, remember?"

Everyone says that before Dad died, he planned to build us a house on his family's land. I'm going to finish what he started.

"Are you excited for the Barrio Fiesta?" Alexa's mom asks. "It's such fun."

"You should invite Jack Allen," Alexa says. I elbow her and she snickers.

For the rest of the meal Alexa and her parents joke and laugh and eat rubbery non-cheese in their cozy, interesting home. I'm glad I came. I feel better now.

Maybe another way I'm like my mom is that sometimes we both wish for a different kind of life.

Alexa's right; I'm probably worried for nothing.

"I propose a toast. To Lou's tiny

house," Alexa says, and we clink our glasses.

CHAPTER 4
ON A MISSION

Finally, the first official day of summer break. I rush out of the house, turn a cartwheel down the sidewalk, and stick my landing right as Manang Maribel and Manang Sheryl drive up to the curb. "Ta-da!" I shout.

"School's out!" Sheryl yells as I get into the car.

"Hey, Louie," Maribel says.

"Hi, *manangs.*"

Maribel is the coolest seventeen-year-old I know, because Auntie let her get a teeny-tiny diamond nose ring — and she can drive. It's strange to think that in a couple years Maribel will be the same age my mom was when she had me.

We're taking a field trip to a place that makes me feel inspired: Annie's Salvage Yard, a large cement lot full of junk and treasures. I work there once a month as my sort-of-a-job. Normally Maribel drops me off on her way to volunteer at the Humane Society. She wants to be a vet one day.

My main task at Annie's is to keep her company while we dream up new ideas for our 1,001 Cool Things to Build List. Like #424, the world's largest catapult. I also help go through the mail and point customers toward the bathroom, that kind of thing. In exchange, I get first dibs on house parts. It's a materials heaven.

Mom lets me work there because she and Annie are old friends, and Mom says she thinks having a job will teach me to be responsible. I think the real reason is because it's like free babysitting.

Today at Annie's is different: We're on a mission.

My family came up with the idea to

charge for jeepney jaunts around the senior center during the festival. In the Philippines, jeepneys are old military jeeps covered with trinkets or decked out in different themes. They're traveling works of art, the flashier the better. An uncle donated his old jeep to the festival, and today we'll find decorations to make it shine.

As we walk into the yard, Sheryl says, "Look for anything silver or sparkly," and she zigzags through rows of things that catch the light and glint.

Little jingle bells chime as we walk into the office. Annie sits behind the counter staring at the computer, probably at cute videos of hedgehogs snoring. She's wearing her uniform of overalls and crazy socks with funky clogs.

Annie's the one who taught me that if I build my house on top of a trailer bed, like the one that's already on my land, the city won't make me pay for an expensive permit. So all I need today is wood. I've been saving up.

"Hi, ladies," Annie says, smiling at us.

"School's finally out." Sheryl pops a

peppermint disk from a tray on the counter into her mouth.

"Hooray!" Annie grabs a couple of old wooden milk crates and hands them over. "Okay, Lou, show your cousins where to look. You can fill these up."

"Sounds good," Maribel says, and she and Annie bump fists.

We snake through a labyrinth of old furniture, car scraps, and oddly shaped metal sculptures that Annie welded together.

This yard is full of things that came from someplace else, so they all have stories behind them. One day my house will have a story behind it, too.

Sheryl stretches out a bunch of flattened soda cans strung together. "What about this?"

"Sure, why not," Maribel says, and Sheryl throws it into a crate with a clunk.

"Hey, can I show you something?" I say. I lead them toward a covered pile in a corner and lift the plastic. "Special sneak peek. House parts."

I point out all the materials I've worked

hard for, like a stainless-steel kitchen sink (not a single dent!) and some pretty brass drawer handles that might have lived in some old San Francisco Edwardian. I've been eyeing thin strips of sugar maple in a dreamy cream color to use for my floor.

"That's exciting. You've been talking about your house forever," Maribel says. I've read every blog, watched every video, and even taken a free planning class on-line.

The girls move on to pick through other rows, but I walk straight toward the wood piles. Long rows of reclaimed hardwoods and softwoods line the fence in short stacks, too many for me to name since there are more than one hundred thousand kinds.

A truck is parked there — with a man loading up my sugar maple.

I run and shout, "Hey, you can't take that!"

"Excuse me?" He closes the back of his truck.

"That's my *floor.*"

The man looks my way. "Sorry, little girl, but Annie just sold it to me." He pats my head, gets in, and drives off.

Little girl?

That sugar maple sat on the lot for months. I thought we'd never sell it. I kick the closest thing, a pile of hubcaps, and they scatter.

"Everything okay, Miss Lou-Lou?" asks Fernando, one of Annie's workers.

The girls sprint over. "What happened?" Sheryl asks.

"I was going to buy that wood! I've been saving all my allowance."

I watch my floor leave the lot, dust trailing in small puffs as the truck rolls away. Fernando smiles at me and says, "Don't worry. I'll help you find something even better."

"Yeah, there's all kinds of wood here, Lou." Maribel says.

I picture Dad's old sketchbook. Mom gave it to me, and on the last page, in big block letters and his messy guy's handwriting, he wrote *Sometimes plans change.* He probably meant things like this.

Fernando and the girls know I can do

this. Together we stack the hubcaps back into a tall tower of metal pancakes.

When Maribel drops me at home, our garage door is wide open. Mom is inside, surrounded by boxes and big plastic bins. She's getting organized for the festival's rummage sale.

"See you at Lola's party tonight!" Maribel beeps and Mom waves as she drives off.

"How'd it go at Annie's?" she asks.

I think about telling her what happened with my wood, but I'm not ready.

"We found a bunch of jeepney decorations."

"Oh, good." Mom reaches toward a top shelf and I go over to help. "Thanks, sweetie," she says as we lower a suitcase. I notice our laptop open and resting on a box, showing an airline site with cheery passengers high up in the clouds.

"Are you going somewhere?"

"I am. It's something I wanted to talk to you about. You have a minute?"

"Sure."

Mom dusts off her hands and sits on the doorstep. "I have some really big news, Lou," she says, smiling. "I was offered a job."

"Wow! That's great. Which hospital? The one in Oakland?"

"No, the one in Washington State we were talking about." She's still smiling, but avoiding my eyes.

Exactly what I was afraid of.

"And you turned them down, right?"

"Oh, sweetheart, not exactly . . ."

I feel my face crumple. "Are we moving?"

Mom wraps an arm around me and gives a tight squeeze. "Not quite yet. I haven't made a final decision, but I do need to give them an answer soon. I booked a flight to check things out."

"Why can't you get a local job?"

"I'm still waiting to hear back from hospitals here," she says. Her face lights up. "Hey, you know how you want your own room? If we move, we'll find our own house, not an apartment. We'll decorate it however we want."

"But I'm going to *build* my own house. Here."

Mom takes my hand and looks at me. "Lou, a great-paying job in a more affordable place will open up all kinds of doors. Remember the taxes I have to pay on your land every year? With a job like this, it won't be as hard. Then, when you're older, you can build your house, I promise. Does that make sense?"

"Not really," I say, and her smile fades.

"I know this isn't what you wanted to hear, honey, but this could be a wonderful opportunity for both of us." She gets up and shuts the laptop. "I booked a red-eye for after the party tonight. I'll only be gone two days, and when I get back we'll figure everything out, okay?"

I nod, but I don't look at her.

"We should get going so we can be early for once," she says, even though we're always on Filipino time. Late.

CHAPTER 5
IN ON A SECRET

Tonight we celebrate Lola's sixty-eighth birthday, although most people think she's a lot younger. It reminds me of my favorite tree fact: The older a tree gets, the faster it grows. The longer Lola lives, the more lively she seems.

Mom and I get into the car. I carefully hold a box on my lap. Inside sits a bright purple, *ube*-flavored spongey cake with white icing, rainbow sprinkles, and glittery candles. We had to buy five packages of candles to make sure we'd have enough.

We're throwing her big bash at a different *lola's* house — Lola Juaning, my grandmother's sister who lives in Daly City.

"Did you girls meet any interesting customers at Annie's today?" Mom asks as she drives. She's perky, but I don't feel like talking.

She tries again. "How's the *bahay kubo* coming along?"

I stare out the window.

Mom glances from the road to me. Finally, she turns on the radio. My family's so loud, I don't think they know what it means to just sit and listen to nothing.

Whenever I'm mad at her, I think about how different my life would be if I had a dad, too. He'd take me for ice cream and walks on the beach, and we'd have secret jokes and signals like my friends do with their dads. Sometimes I hang out with my uncles, tagging along when they're out with my cousins, but it's not really the same.

The aunties always bother Mom about

getting married. We do our best to ignore them. She dates, but there's no one special.

My parents met at an art and design college in San Francisco. Dad majored in architecture, like I will one day, and Mom studied interior design. They had a plan. He'd create buildings and she'd make them beautiful inside. But obviously, that never happened. When Mom got pregnant, Lola and Lolo made her leave art school and get a job. Filipinos didn't study interior design. They were practical professionals, like nurses and teachers and certified med techs.

My dad's mother, Grandma Beverly, passed away a long time ago. Mom and I never knew her. I do remember Grandpa Ted, the happiest man with the strongest hug. I can still feel his arms around me whenever I think of him.

Right after I was born, Mom and I went to live in Grandpa Ted's guesthouse, a one-room studio where I felt safe and cozy. I think it counted as my first tiny house. Everyone says that our living with Grandpa Ted helped him cope with the tragedy as much as it did Mom and me.

Lola likes to tell the story of how she and Lolo thought they didn't have anything in common with my white grandpa, but it turns out they did — a love for their kids.

I never knew the difference between my white grandpa and my brown one because they loved me the same. Being half and half is something I don't think about much. A lot of my friends at school are a mix of all kinds of people. Sometimes I get asked "What are you?" It's a silly question. I always say "I'm me."

Grandpa Ted died when I was almost six, so we went to live with Lolo and Lola. I missed Grandpa Ted, but Lolo and Lola comforted me with their stories and hugs, and with the dishes they cooked that made their house smell so good.

I own two things of the Nelsons' — their land and my not-so-Filipino features. I'm taller and have lighter hair and skin than my cousins, with a pointier nose and eyes that only sometimes look Asian. When I'm around them, it's easy to see I'm only half. Once, in Golden Gate Park, someone asked Mom how long she'd been my nanny. She got so mad. Still, Mom knows that inside I'm just as Filipina as she is. We connect with each other no matter how different we look.

Finally, we reach Daly City. A lot of Filipinos live here. You can find *calamansi* juice and green beans for stewing at the farmers market, or a ton of Filipino restaurants and shops. I always spot people who look like my family, and get a feeling of home.

Mom parks in the steep driveway of Lola Juaning's house.

"Lou, honey, I'm sorry if I upset you. Let's go in and enjoy the party." She smiles at me, but I don't want to look her in the eye.

She's serious about moving, and I have to do something about it. But what?

Think, Lou.

We get out of the car and pause long enough to notice the sun slung low, pink clouds piled high. And suddenly, my brain sprouts a plan.

At the doorway Mom slips off her sandals and I fling my flip-flops onto a mountain of shoes. Younger cousins are planted on the couch playing video games, while uncles and *lolos* drink San Miguel beer and argue about corrupt Philippine politics. People belt out sappy love songs around the karaoke machine, and all the aunties in the kitchen make *chismis,* gossip. The house surrounds me with the familiar noises of a big room holding a family I love.

A long table in the dining room has all my favorite dishes: crispy *lumpia* rolls, clear *pancit* noodles, and sweet and sticky banana *turon.* "Go eat, go eat," says Lola Juaning — the first words I hear when I walk into any Filipino party.

Sometimes this mix of sounds and smells overwhelms me, but when it's gone, I kind of miss it.

"What took you guys so long?" Sheryl says. "Uncle Benny's on his fifth version of 'Dancing Queen.' "

"Meeting time," I say. She grabs two

sodas and a handful of *lumpias,* and I pull her outside.

We sit on the curb, flicking open our cans and watching some cousins play hockey. They grip their sticks and smack a black puck back and forth across the street, until one of them shouts, "Car!" and they scatter. Once the car's out of sight, the game's back on.

Sheryl hands me a *lumpia,* freshly fried. I crunch in, and juice from the veggies and meat bursts in my mouth.

"What's so important?" she asks.

"Only the worst possible thing." I spill the whole story.

She shoves the last inch of roll into her mouth and mumbles, "Wow, it'd be so strange if you didn't live near us anymore."

"Not gonna happen. I came up with the best idea."

"Uh-oh."

"You know my tiny house?"

"You mean *our* tiny house? I get my own reading nook, remember?"

"Yup. I'm going to build it this summer, and then Mom won't want to take that job."

Sheryl gives me her I-don't-believe-you face. "Exactly how's that supposed to work?"

"Well, when Mom sees what I've made by myself, she'll want to stay. She's always talking about my land being my future and how it's supposed to help with college and all that. So if I put a house there, she'll see that my future's right here."

The more I talk about it, the more sense it makes.

And now the thoughts rush in: adjusting the blueprints, prepping the trailer bed, lounging on the finished deck with my friends while sipping lemonade from fancy glasses. But the best part? The look of pride on Mom's face when she sees it.

"That's it! I'll surprise her!"

Sheryl's not excited. "Louie, do you even know how to build a house?"

"Sure. I've built lots of things."

"Wooden flip-flops don't count." I liked that idea, until the principal called Lola to come bring me regular shoes. My invention was too noisy for school.

"I have to at least give it a shot." I don't see any other way.

"You should convince your mom to get a job someplace more exciting, like . . . Disneyland! I'd visit."

"Don't say anything about my plan yet, okay? If Mom hears, she'll make me stop, and I need some time to get the house up for this to work."

One of the aunties shouts from the doorway, "Cake time, kids!"

"Let's go light the candles." Sheryl springs from the curb and dusts off her bottom. She offers a hand and lifts me.

Sheryl and I push sixty-eight candles into creamy icing, packing them in tight. I light two and we use those to tag-team the rest, racing to finish before the wax drips. We carry the cake out on a silver tray, lit and sparkling.

Lola sits at the table, her black-and-gray hair pulled back in a low bun and a crown of flowers topping her head. Everyone holds up phones to take pictures. Flashes blink like fireworks, and we sing at the top of our lungs, *"Haaaaaappy biiiiirthday tooooo yoooou!"*

Sheryl glances at me and I smile: We're in on a secret now.

After the party we drive back to Lola Celina's house. Uncle Jon-Jon, Sheryl and Maribel's dad, carries in large bags packed with gifts. Lola asked us not to bring presents, but for once nobody followed her orders. Anyway, I can tell she wanted them, because she's giddy, clapping her hands like a little kid as Uncle dumps her loot into a bright pyramid.

"Let's open them!" Lola says.

"I'll help!" Sheryl says.

Great. I wanted quiet time to get ready for my first day of building, but they'll never leave now.

Mom clears her throat and says, "Okay, family, before Lola starts, I have an official announcement to make."

"You finally found a boyfriend?" Lola says, joking, although kind of not.

Oh no. They're only going to be encouraging, and that won't help me at all.

"Better. I was offered the job in Washington."

"Congratulations!" Auntie Gemma jumps up to hug Mom and they giggle, until Auntie stands back and peers at her. "Gosh, when you said you were looking outside the Bay Area, I didn't think you were serious."

"We'll see, but I actually think the time's right, Manang. I'd have a great salary, so Lou and I could save up. They'd even pay for grad school. Those are huge benefits."

The sisters start fast-chattering the way they do whenever they're excited. Even Maribel joins in. "I could apply to colleges there."

Lola interrupts her daughters by wrapping her arms around their waists. "Minda, we haven't discussed what this would mean for the family."

"Oh, Mom, I love you, but I don't think this is a group decision."

Lola looks hurt, although Mom's probably right. "*Anak,* we don't have any close relatives there. And what will you do about Lou? Who will cook her shrimp and peel them for her?" Lola smiles my way. "Who will be home for her when you're working?"

"And what about *me*?" Sheryl adds. "I don't want Lou to go!"

"I don't want Lou to go, either!" I say.

Mom laughs. "Oh, sweeties . . ."

"It's only a two-hour flight. We'd get to do a lot of fun girls' trips," Auntie says.

"Just think about what it would mean to take Lou from her family — can you do that?" Lola asks.

I hate it when grown-ups talk about kids while we're in the room, like we're not smart enough to know what's going on.

"Can we please open gifts now?" I say.

"Gladly," Lola says. I hand her a sparkly box and she tears into it.

There's only one spot in Lola's house that I can call my own: the bedroom closet. Mom gave it to me. It's a walk-in, big enough to fit my clothes and books and me sitting crisscross with our family laptop.

It's finally quiet in the house.

I yank on the light chain in my closet. On the wall in front of me hangs a vision heart.

Maribel's vision board gave me the idea. Hers is big and glittery with pictures of the things she wants in her life, like dreamy movie stars for boyfriends, or dollar signs, or colleges she's trying to get into. She stares at it every single night. Supposedly, if you look at the things you want, they'll show up in real life: *Blink!*

My board has pictures of family and friends, and in between the spaces, holding it together, are tiny houses in all shapes and colors, cut out from magazines. There are also different sayings, like *Be You-nique* or *Pretty in Pink but Wicked with a Hammer* or (my favorite) *Tiny Is Big.*

Tonight Mom leaves for Washington, tomorrow I have dance practice, and the day after that — building time.

I stare at my heart and slowly inhale, slowly exhale. It helps me focus. Yes. Focus and get to work.

CHAPTER 6
PROVING MYSELF WRONG

"Okay, dancers, let's try this again, but on the beat this time," says Miss Jovy, a little panicky. She freaks out when we mess up. Barrio Fiesta's in a little over a month, but we're still getting the hang of our dance. It's a hard one.

Onstage, Cody and I take our places. The music starts, and we hop into a set of giant clapping bamboo poles on the floor. The dancers next to us jump on the wrong beat and trip. Miss Jovy smacks her hand to her forehead.

This is the first time I get to dance *Tinikling,* a folk dance that mimics a tikling bird hopping between stems of grass and running over tree branches.

The dance works like this: pole holders lay long, thick bamboo poles flat onto the stage. They bounce them on the floor twice, then clap them together. It makes a sharp beat, a rhythmic song: *bounce bounce click, bounce bounce click, bounce click click, bounce bounce click.*

Then the music starts, and dancers like me and Cody hop and twirl our way through the clapping reeds. At least, that's how it's supposed to happen, but only if everyone stays synchronized, which seems impossible with so many poles and feet moving, and clumsy cousins like Arwin, who still gets his ankles caught. The music starts slow, then speeds up crazy fast. Sheryl's so glad she doesn't have to dance in this one. Alexa says it's kind of like a huge Filipino version of double Dutch, but without the jump ropes.

Miss Jovy is a pretty Filipina college student studying biology, and she's also in charge of her university's PCN, or Pilipino Cultural Night. That's a whole night of folk dancing, just like this, at colleges all over the country. My favorite numbers are the ones where the dancers balance candles on their heads.

Now our music has stopped. We're tired and want to go home, but Miss Jovy says, "Let's try it without the music this time." I stand next to the pole holders and wait for our signal. "Ready . . . one two three, one two three, hop turn turn, hop skip skip . . ."

Cody and I are the only ones who make it through without tripping. Success!

"Wow, nice job, Lou." Miss Jovy pats my shoulder. I didn't think I could do it. I like proving myself wrong.

Today's the day.

Mom and Lola think I'm at Sheryl's, and Sheryl said she'd cover. But before I go, I'll need something. I peek into the garage. Lolo's old black tool cabinet sits dusty in the corner, as tall as I am.

I slide open the drawers, starting with the top and working my way down.

I see screwdrivers and screws.

Measuring tape and levels.

Small parts and metal things.

Finally, in the last one, I find what I need — pliers and a crowbar. I slip them into my backpack.

I'm pretty sure no one who lives in San Francisco likes driving. It's easiest to take the bus, so most of the time that's what Mom and I do. We barely use our car. I know all the routes by heart, like the one that travels across the Golden Gate Bridge into Terra Vista Valley, the small town where my land lives. That's Route 143, one stop, no transfers.

I've never gone out there alone — until now.

I'm nervous, not because I'm scared or I might get lost, but because Mom doesn't know. She gets back from Washington late today and if she finds out, it will finish this plan. If someone stops me because I'm alone, I'll say my parents are waiting for me at the other end. Then I'll fake-sneeze and make gross phlegmy sounds so they'll back off.

The bus hisses at the curb where I'm

waiting, and the doors swing open. I step on and toss in some quarters with a clink. The driver doesn't even glance my way. Easy.

I choose a seat in the middle where there's no one sitting near me except for a lady with a baby, who studies me for a few seconds. I give a small smile and stare down at my Converse.

Sunshine pours in through the windows and the bus chugs on its way. Soon I'm smiling. I can't believe I'm going out there like this. Mom's away and Lola's out — I have the whole day.

We pass through the Rainbow Tunnel, with its archway painted in all seven colors of the rainbow. At the end, the bay sparkles below. Not far now.

Chapter 7
A Tiny House
in the Woods

When the bus reaches the hillside, I'm the only one who steps off. I'm in front of the park where Grandpa Ted used to take me, where we imagined building tree houses high up in the redwoods' top branches.

The sky still has its dawnlike blush. Early-morning light feels magical, like I can do anything.

It's always sunrise somewhere. John Muir said that. He was a guy who had a gigantic grove of redwoods named after him, called Muir Woods, where we take school trips every year. Some redwoods are over a thousand years old, as tall as skyscrapers. I drop my head back and stare straight up. I don't mind feeling small when the giants are trees.

This is another place where great ideas pop into my head, with nothing crowding me but nature, and air that feels good on my arms.

Across the way is the town's main street with mailboxes nailed to a wooden post, a pizza place, and a convenience store with a sign that usually says Closed. Around me, a few trails vein off into the hillside. Sometimes they stretch to hidden houses, like they will to mine one day.

It's chilly, and my breath comes out in small puffs. I slip on a fleece and start the short trek up.

The first time I found out about my land, I was eight. It started with a question: "Mommy, what was Daddy like?"

She said, "I want to take you someplace."

We drove there, winding around hills I

somewhat knew — Grandpa Ted's old house wasn't far. Finally, we landed in a secret spot where trees and sunlight came together. As soon as we stepped out, I wanted to sit still and listen.

"Where are we?"

"Where you can remember the Nelsons. This belongs to you, Lou."

What did? The trees? The plants? The dirt under my feet?

"We used to hike around here with Grandpa Ted, remember?" she said. "He gave all this to you, even that shed over there."

Mom showed me where the property started and ended, with rows of bushes like fences. So many sounds of bugs and the wind blowing leaves. She fanned out a picnic blanket for lunch while I found the shallow creek and learned how chilly and perfect the water felt on my feet. My land had other things, too, like an orange hammock connecting two trees, and a rusty old trailer bed.

"There's something else. Cover your eyes, and don't peek. It's a surprise."

When she said, "Look!" a wooden dollhouse sat on the ground. I crouched down and peered in. It had a kitchen, stairs, and a bedroom with a miniature bed and a real cloth blanket.

"Did you buy this for me?"

"No, your dad built this for you when we were in college. Isn't it beautiful?"

The dollhouse had two teeny wooden rockers with a little doll sitting in each: one with light brown hair like mine, and the other with pitch-black hair like Mom's. I couldn't wait to show them to Sheryl, who had always wanted a Barbie with black hair to match her own (she had to color her Barbie's head with black marker).

"Why didn't you bring me here before?"

"I wanted to wait until you could take good care of it. This will be for you one day when you're ready. It's a gift to help with your future. Our family treasure."

The dollhouse made me so happy, but Mom seemed upset. She sat and hugged her knees.

"Did I do something wrong?"

"No, sweetie pie, I'm remembering.

This is where your dad asked me to marry him."

"And that makes you sad?"

She shook her head. "Happy, but . . . I miss him, that's all."

At least she had memories — I didn't have any.

Mom brightened. "Want to hear something? He was going to build a house for us. You were going to have your own playroom, and I was going to have my own art studio." She took my hand and led me around, describing their big dreams. "Your grandpa Ted worked in construction, and they were going to build it together, right on this very spot." She beamed at it.

"Let's do it ourselves! Let's build a house here!" I said, but she only laughed.

The rest of the day we played with the dollhouse while I dreamed of a tiny house in the woods.

I keep walking, snapping a few pictures of a madrone tree with its papery orange bark flaking away from the trunk, the new skin underneath yellow-green and satiny smooth. Whenever Lola's come out here, she's taught me about living things.

The path ends in a flat clearing surrounded by more redwoods. All around, crooked branches like witches' fingers make patterns where the sun crisscrosses through.

In the Philippines, my grandparents had acres of fields where they raised tobacco plants with wide, full leaves. Lolo said that before harvest time, the leaves would grow to the height of a short man. You could see for miles over them, until your eyes reached a line of shadowy mountains topped by sky.

I throw my backpack on a pile of leaves and unpeel a plastic tarp that covers the trailer bed. What peeks out is a large, flat grid of metal beams with thick wheels and a sturdy triangle at the front, the tongue, for hitching. This trailer bed is rusty and old, but it'll work. People who build tiny houses from scratch use them as the foundation.

I read about a family who got rid of almost everything they had, and kept only enough to fit into a camper while they roamed the country. They didn't want expensive things, only memories. I like the idea that a house can be anywhere, because a home is about more than the stuff we buy to stick inside.

Something rustles. I peer around to make sure it's not a skunk; then I see a fuzzy squirrel race up a tree. They like to feed on the seeds of evergreens.

I cover the trailer bed.

My family used to picnic here, and the cousins and I would catch minnows at the creek. Lolo always brought ripe mangoes; he'd score lines into the flesh so we could flip the halves open and eat the sweet cubes. I asked him if we could grow a mango tree, but he said my land was too dry for that. Still, we dug a hole near the shed and planted the pit, just to try.

Lolo taught me that gardening means imagining things before they happen, like where to root the plants, what's needed to keep them alive, and how they'll add to your view someday — kind of like planning a house.

Whenever we came to my land, the aunties would tell Mom to look in the shed, but she didn't have a key. Lola would remind them that they shouldn't search through dead people's things; it would only bring bad luck.

I've never seen it open, but if Dad and Grandpa Ted wanted to build on this spot, here's my guess: It'll have all the things I need.

The shed has a padlock joined onto an old metal strip. With the pliers from Lolo's tool cabinet, I try to pull off the lock, but it doesn't budge. Next, I try the crowbar. I slip it behind the strip and pull down as hard as I can — it shifts the teeniest bit. I keep prying and prying until the strip moves a little more.

It's working.

I use as much muscle power as I can until the whole piece drops, lock and all.

The wooden doors swing open slightly, and it's dark inside. I thought I'd rush in, but it feels kind of weird. What if Lola's right and I'm disturbing their spirits? But they're my family; they love me. They won't mind.

Go for it, Lou. The shed's yours, too.

I take a deep breath and pull open the doors.

Sunlight floods a dusty space with nests of cobwebs in the corners. The shed has a worktable piled high with stuff and a giant Peg-Board wall with lots of tools hanging from silver hooks. I see hammers, pliers, tape rolls, measuring sticks, drills, scissors . . .

Holy. Cow. It's an entire hardware store! I scream and jump around and it makes the dust fly.

On the table sits a box with a name on it in big messy black letters: *Michael Nelson.* I recognize the handwriting from his sketchbooks.

I approach it carefully, like it's enchanted — and I touch the box, too. I close my eyes and try to feel us connecting on this spot where he stood.

Should I open it?

Gently, I lift the cover. The box is packed with bulky black rectangles — old movie tapes, I think. Lola has a shelf of Filipino movies that look the same, but these have blank labels, so I'm not sure what they are. I'm putting them back in their places when something on the opposite wall catches my attention.

Jackpot!

Long planks of wood rest along the wall, bundled in tight stacks, a ton of them, sitting on top of each other. I can't believe it. I'm sure there's enough to build the framework of my house, probably even enough for the floor.

I grab the end of a bundle, but it's so heavy I can barely inch it up. Something skitters out and sweeps past my hands. A tiny black mouse runs into sunlight.

Okay, Lou. Breathe. You got this.

On the Peg-Board wall hang garden clippers, like Lola's. I snip the plastic ties around the wood. Easy.

I slide off the top plank and walk backward with it, but stumble and fall right on my bum. It's taller than I am and super heavy, so I drag it out into the daylight. I want a better look.

The wood's light-colored, with soft gray grain running down it like pathways. It's raw, not varnished. I swipe my hand over its surface and a splinter pricks my finger. It stings as I pluck it out.

The mouse skitters close, nibbling from its hands.

"Hey, little guy. You here to help?"

I stare into the shed at all the stacks of wood I'll need to move. Building a house might be harder than I thought.

Maybe it's time for a break — or some inspiration — and I know just the thing. It's still early; I can always come back.

I leave the plank, close the shed, and grab my backpack before walking down to the stop; the bus comes right as I arrive, opening its doors like an invitation.

We roll through the hills and I rest my head on the window. It's a little fogged up, so I draw a smiley face.

The bus stops in Sausalito, a charming touristy town Mom and I visit to eat bowls of clam chowder and stroll along the water. It also has one of my favorite things: houseboats.

We pull up to the curb and I hop off.

CHAPTER 8
NO ONE ELSE KNOWS

It's a perfect day, with sailboats dotting the bay. I'm in the middle of a good people-watching spot, on a busy block of fancy stores. This main street will take me to the water.

It feels friendlier here than in the city. Gum doesn't blotch the sidewalks, it doesn't smell like pee, and there aren't areas to avoid once the sun sets. It's a good thinking place.

Along the bay, paddleboarders balance, pushing forward with oars while cormorants float around them. One of the birds dips in and pops up again with a fish in its bill. Out here something in the water's always moving, making patterns, changing.

The rows of houseboats sit anchored near faded wooden docks, and each one's a little different. I take photos all around: an herb garden planted in a giant cowboy boot; bicycles chained to the fences; a nautical steering wheel hung on a rail, splitting the sun into triangles on the ground. A cat saunters to a bowl of water left outside of someone's bright green door.

I love it out here. Ideas stream into my head.

"Lou from Nubby's class?" says a voice.

A boy who looks like Jack Allen walks out of a houseboat. It *is* Jack Allen. What's he doing here?

"Oh, hey," I try to say like it's no big deal, the way Alexa or Sheryl might act around a boy.

"I saw you from my window. I thought that was you. Why are you taking pictures of my house?"

His house?

"Do you live in one of these?"

"Sort of. That one." He points to a blue houseboat a few feet from us. "I'm here with my dad and John. Our neighbors call us the three boat bachelors."

Jack has an older brother in high school, and they look alike except that John's taller, stockier, and more jocklike. The eighth-grade girls love it when he picks Jack up from school.

"These houseboats are super cool," I say, to avoid his question.

"Technically it's not a houseboat."

"What do you mean?"

"Because there's no motor. It's a floating home."

"Oh," I say. "Right." I give him a smile. I don't want to seem dumb.

"Have you ever been inside one?" I shake my head. And then — amazing! — he says, "You wanna come in?"

I bite my lip and glance around to see if Carver Jamison or anyone else from the popular group is hiding out, in case they're playing some sort of mean joke.

But we're alone. For a second I almost say no — he makes me too nervous — but I can't not see the inside of a house on the water.

"Yeah, sure, that'd be great. I mean, sure, I guess."

We're standing at Jack Allen's front door.

The girls. Are going. To freak.

"How can you live on a boat? Doesn't it get all rocky?" I ask.

"Duh, it's just like a normal house." He opens the door.

Inside, it's small but cheerful. There's a couch and TV in the living room. Plants hang in the corners to "bring in some nature," as Lola would say. A spiral staircase leads up to a second level. I knew floating homes could have more than one story, but it's different to see it in real life. It feels homey, like a place where I'd want to hang out and play board games.

"I like it. It's so cute in here," I say.

"If cute means small, then you're right. There's no room for anything extra."

Kind of like a tiny house. He walks in

deeper, and I'm not sure if I should follow. He was probably only trying to seem polite.

"Does your mom live with you guys?" I ask. He didn't mention her earlier.

"Nope. She's in France somewhere with her rich French husband. I've never been there and she never comes to see us anymore," he says, matter-of-fact.

So Jack's a guy with a mom and a dad but not both at once. That's still probably better than never having known one of your parents.

"Do you miss her?"

"I remember in summers we'd spend the whole day having water-gun fights. I miss stuff like that." He looks off as he says this. I probably brought up something too sad for him to think about.

"My dad's not around, either," I say.

"Are your parents divorced, too?"

"No, he died before I was born."

"Oh, wow, sorry," Jack says.

"Thanks, it's okay," I say. "Hey, how come you go to school in the city but live all the way out here?"

"I don't. This is where my dad lived before John and I were born. We come on the weekends."

"Where are they?"

"My dad's out for a run. Not sure about John. I'm staying in to work."

"Where do you work?" I picture Jack as a friendly nature-camp counselor for cute little preschoolers, where they all wear the same shirt and he has a catchy name like Juniper-Berry Jack and carries trail mix in his pockets for them.

"I'll show you," he says. "Just don't make fun of me."

I should probably remind him that our entire school made fun of *me* because of the nickname he started. But I don't, because I might discover something about Jack Allen that no one else knows.

We wind up the stairs, passing a wall of framed photos. There's one of the baby Allen brothers as Halloween pumpkins. Oh my goodness, so sweet. There's another of Jack and his dad — Jack's holding one of those black-and-white clapper boards that movie directors use when they shout "Take one!"

His dad has black hair and darker skin than Jack, but they have the same eyes and nose. There's also a picture of a woman with light skin and hair who somehow looks like Jack, too — his mom. So he's a mix, like me.

I'd like to see all the pictures, but I don't want him to think I have a crush on him. We don't have time, anyway, since we're walking right into his bedroom.

Jack. Allen's. Bedroom!

My friends will never believe this.

Jack's room has light blue walls. His bed isn't made, and there are crumpled clothes all over. A poster of *The Goonies* hangs lopsided on the wall, and his desk sits under a big window with a view of other floating houses. People in skinny red kayaks row past, and I wave to them. What a cool place to live.

"Here it is, my million-dollar masterpiece." Jack points to three large computer screens on the desk, attached by a wad of tangled cords.

He sits down and types into a keyboard.

An image jumps out, of sailboats gliding along the bay on a pretty day.

"I'm making a promo video for Frank's Diner," he says.

"Was that for media? I thought shop was your elective."

"It's not for school, it's sort of my hobby. Frank knows my dad, and he hired me to make a commercial for their website. I want to go to UCLA and study filmmaking and win an Oscar one day."

I never thought of Jack as artsy.

A video plays, with customers chowing down and saying how much they love Frank's spicy gluten-free kimchi breakfast burritos.

"You sold me. I'd eat there."

"John thinks making movies is for geeks, but I don't. There's this film camp my dad said I could go to in L.A. — you stay in dorm rooms and everything — but I have to apply with a short movie or documentary. I'm going to make it this summer so I can send it in the fall."

"What's it going to be about?"

He shrugs. "Not sure yet."

I tell him how it's too bad we're not in Hong Kong because then he could film the Aberdeen Floating Village. It has ancient Chinese sailing ships called junks, hundreds clustered together with thousands of people living in them. Behind them, there's a skyline of shining high-rises.

"I'd like to see that," Jack says.

"I wish I knew how to edit catchy videos. I want to post some to teach other kids how to build stuff."

"The Lou Channel," he says. "Do-it-yourself at its finest."

Jack stays at his desk and I sit on the edge of his bed, and here's another surprise: We keep talking, about all kinds of things. Movies and floating homes and his brother's pranks, like last night when John wore a scary clown mask and tapped Jack while he was asleep. The neighbors came over because of all the screaming. They both got busted.

Jack's a performer, waving his arms around and using goofy expressions to tell his stories, and it makes me crack up. Now I see why everyone likes him. Sitting here, talking about whatever, he's not intimidating like other popular kids.

"How come you're so good at shop class?" he asks.

No one's ever wanted to know that before. "I probably get it from my dad and grandpas. They were all handy. Plus, I used to take Woodworking for Kids at the Y, but it got canceled because some parent complained about the dangers of using tools, which is ridiculous because organized sports are way more hazardous."

"Yeah, like the time I got smacked in dodgeball and lost a tooth." He opens his mouth and points to the fake replacement, a little whiter than all the rest.

"Thanks for sharing," I say, and we laugh. "I don't know. I guess I like seeing when I transform ideas from my head into real-life things. It's kind of hard to explain."

"That's how I feel about making movies," he says.

Jack Allen and I have more in common than I ever would have guessed. I decide to take a chance and tell him my secret. "The reason I was taking pictures out here is for inspiration. I'm building my own house."

"You said that in Nubby's class." He remembered? I didn't think anyone was listening, especially him.

"It's going to be a tiny house."

"Like for Hobbits?"

"No, they're for anyone."

"How tiny's tiny?"

"Way smaller than this houseboat."

"Why would you want to live in something that size? I already feel squished in here. John takes up half the room when we're together."

I count out the reasons on my fingers: "There's the saving-the-planet part because they're more efficient. . . . There's the saving-money part since you wouldn't have a bunch of bills because you're not living in a mansion. . . . Then there's the whole wow factor because, well, you're building a house!"

I'm probably talking too fast and getting too excited, since I can feel my heart thumping. He stares at me like I have a booger hanging from my nose (which I

91

sure hope I don't).

When I stop rattling on, it gets quiet, even though we've been talking back and forth nonstop. Jack jiggles the computer mouse. We've run out of things to say. Now he's going to tell all his friends, *Yup, she's a weirdo.*

"Thanks for showing me your house-boat. I mean, your floating home with no motor," I say, getting up. I hop over a pile of clothes, bolt to the staircase, and spiral down as fast as I can.

"Hold on," he says, following me.

We reach the front door and he's looking at my face. I have to glance away.

"I can't miss my bus."

"Do you hate me?" he asks. It doesn't seem like he's joking.

"For what?"

"Because everyone still calls you President TP."

"Oh yeah . . . that." How could I forget?

"I wish I could take it back."

I can't believe it's something he's thought about.

"It's okay, I forgive you," I say, and his

expression turns into a smile. At me.

Jack Allen's exactly like a floating house — unexpected. I think we count as friends now, even though he gives my stomach the flutters. It's kind of a nice feeling.

CHAPTER 9
SEEING MY DREAM

I board the bus and find a seat. We bump along, and after a short ride, the bus stops at a curb. Passengers step off and on.

A kiosk poster catches my attention: *Go Tiny, Live Large.*

Under the slogan is a picture of a tiny house with a bright red door. It says *Open House, Seven Days a Week,* and there's an address and some hours.

I've seen this poster around the city, and I've always wondered about it. Sheryl once told me she saw a commercial for it and that they sell tiny homes.

The last of the passengers steps down, and the bus doors clamp shut.

"Hold on, please!" I yell, getting up, and once again they open.

I punch the address from the poster into my phone and see that the open house isn't far. Cool. After a few blocks I find myself standing in front of a cottage that's been turned into an office. Before me stretches a whole block of offices that look like gingerbread houses.

A colorful sign greets me: *Welcome Home!*

Inside, the living room's a lobby, with a desk of brochures stacked high and a woman who asks, "May I help you?"

"Uh, hi. My name's Lou, and . . . ummm . . . I saw you were having an open house?" I look around. "I was just wondering . . . What is this place?"

She gives a friendly laugh. "We sell homes here. Tiny ones. There's one out back that folks can tour."

"Seriously? It's my dream to own a tiny house. I'm building one right now."

"That's quite a project."

I shrug. "For some people, maybe, but I'll do it. Except I've never seen one in person before."

"Well, we can definitely change that."

The nice woman takes me through a hallway with old bedrooms turned into offices. Some have people sitting at their desks, and they look up at me and smile as we pass. We end at a door in a kitchen.

"Watch your step," she says, opening it.

We walk into a backyard, but instead of a garden or patio, the yard holds another house, one with a bright red door, sitting on a bed of bark. The same house as in the poster.

"Here she is, our star. One of our most popular models."

I walk up to the structure. It's not much taller than I am. "Do you help people build these?"

"No, it's what's called a prefab. That means it comes fully assembled."

I try to understand. "You mean people

96

don't have to build the house themselves?"

She nods. "We have a few different models to choose from. Our company takes care of the hard part. Then we ship them out and the owners can move right in."

"That sounds much easier than what I'm trying to do," I say, and the woman laughs.

"Would you like to take a look?"

It's a real, physical, finished tiny house. For a second I even have to catch my breath — that same feeling I get after making something I'm proud of. I'm seeing my dream. This is a thousand times better than pictures taped to a vision heart.

The space is a single room with a shelf and small love seat, and a pretty vase of flowers in the kitchen nook. The living area has the kind of table I want to put in my house. "May I?" I ask, and the woman gives me the okay. I bend the legs in and fold the table right into the wall — it works!

I turn in a circle and look around. It's kind of like a dollhouse come to life, and everything's within easy reach.

I'm hit with a memory of my family in Grandpa Ted's guesthouse, an afternoon when we crammed everyone in — Lola, my cousins. One of the uncles brought his guitar and everyone sang and ate, and the cousins played inside and outside, blending the indoors and outdoors so it all seemed like one.

"So, what do you think of this model?" she asks. "Would you live here?"

"It's perfect."

A ladder leads to the sleeping loft, and I climb up, crawl in. A skylight shows off blue sky and clouds. Peering down from up high reminds me of sitting on top of Lolo's shoulders while we'd walk around Barrio Fiesta, seeing things from a new view.

Now I'm even more curious. "How much does a house like this cost?" I ask, climbing down.

"It varies depending on a homeowner's needs, but the base price for this model is about sixty-five thousand dollars."

Oh. My. Gosh. "People actually pay that?"

She laughs. "Yes, we've sold quite a few. Some of our newer models have wait lists."

I ask her more questions and she's not staring at me like I'm loony, only answering the way she might with any adult. She grabs a brochure from the bookshelf and hands it to me.

"It's been wonderful to meet you, Lou. Good luck on your project. You'll have to keep us posted."

Before I leave, I turn around one last time and snap a photo of myself so I can remember all of it.

I head back to the bus stop and think about what I did today — and what I need to do next. It felt great on my land, but now I know for sure: Building my house will take work. Lots of it.

On all my favorite design shows there's an expert who guides the DIYers. I could use an in-person guru to help, instead of me pausing and rewinding how-to videos every few seconds to follow along. If Dad was alive, he'd be that person.

Maybe I could still ask Mr. Keller. He lives in this neighborhood. When Lolo was alive, he and Lola would visit Mr. Keller at his house. I've never been, but he's invited us over before. Lola said she'll take me one day because he lives in someplace unique that she wants me to see.

I pull out my phone and find a website to type in *Peter Keller.* An address pops up, and the map shows me I can easily walk there. Here I go.

CHAPTER 10
ORIGINAL PLAN

Mr. K's house has a bright purple door with a line sawed through the middle, a Dutch door for keeping farm animals out, or kids in. Already it's an interesting place.

I ring the doorbell and a gong sounds. I laugh. He answers and looks surprised. "Oh my, what a pleasant gift! Why, hello, Lucinda!"

I give a cheery wave. "Hi. I was in the neighborhood. Hope it's okay I came by?"

"Of course! Please, come in." He peers behind me. "Where are Celina and Minda?"

"Oh, it's just me," I say, but he doesn't seem concerned.

Once I enter, I notice something strange — that I'm still outside. I'm standing in an open-air courtyard surrounded by enormous sheets of glass panels. I'm not inside the house yet, but I can see right into it.

"Where are the walls?" I ask, and he chuckles.

"You like?"

Mr. Keller slides open the glass and we step into the living room. On the opposite end is more glass, and my view goes straight to the backyard.

"I've never seen a house like this," I say.

"People call them Eichlers, after Joseph Eichler, the builder. He built spaces that felt like you could be indoors and outdoors at the same time."

"Except you have to be careful not to run into the glass when you think it's open but it's actually closed, which I may or may not have done on occasion," says Mr. Keller's partner, Mr. Ko, who walks into the room. Mr. Ko has silver-and-black hair. He used to teach high school English, and Mom says he got everyone to love reading.

"Hi, Mr. Ko, it's great to see you again."

"Ed, you remember Lucinda Bulosan-Nelson?"

"Yes, it's been a while, but I remember you, your mother, and your beautiful names very well — Lucinda and Luzviminda." He gives me a friendly hug.

I got named to kind of match Mom's. Hers is common in the Philippines. It's a mash-up of the three island groups of Luzon, Visayas, and Mindanao. Everyone calls her Minda.

"I've heard about all the excellent work you did in class this year, Lucinda."

"Mr. Ko, you can call me Lou."

"Then you can call me Ed."

"My nickname kind of sounds like a truck driver, but that's what I like about it. It's different."

They both smile at me.

"Speaking of Minda, where is she?" Mr. Keller asks. "Everything all right?"

Hmmm. I didn't think this through. I can tell the truth about how I went out to my land this morning, or I can lie about it. No matter what I tell him, he'll probably report back to Mom. Either way, she'll find out.

"Oh, everything's fine. She's not with me right now. Letting kids do things by themselves is called free-range parenting. So we can learn to make good choices."

This is not a lie. It's how Alexa's mom thinks. Alexa gets to do all kinds of things without her parents worrying. In my family, none of us are even allowed to date until *after college.* Maribel had to beg her parents to let her go to Fall Formal, and they only said yes because she got into all AP classes.

Mr. Keller pauses. "What an excellent idea to learn how to navigate the world, don't you think, Ed?" he says. *Phew.*

"Was this house built in the mid-century?" I ask.

"You seem to know a lot about architecture," Ed says.

"I watch the Home Channel with Lola. It's our thing. Plus, I have my dad's old sketchbooks with all his house designs." I'm glad I do. His doodles and notes helped me get to know him better.

"Want to hear something else interesting?" Mr. Keller points to walls of solid wood. "This is *luan,* a type of mahogany from the Philippines. It's what the original houses were made from."

I slide my palm across the warm reddish color and try to imagine the trees they came from. Filipino walls. My cousins will want to hear this.

I think it's true that dog owners can resemble their pets, like a guy with shaggy hair and a droopy face might have a dog with shaggy fur and a droopy face. It's the same with people's homes. Where they live can echo them. If your place is cluttered, well, probably you're feeling that way, too — that's happened to me at Lola's.

In class we always know when Mr. Keller's mad (nostrils puff up and nose hairs stick out), curious (eyes squint), or happy (whistles while working). You see right into him. This glass house suits him perfectly.

"Lou, may I interest you in some iced tea and a slice of my famous strawberry-rhubarb pie?" Ed asks.

"No, thank you. But I was wondering . . . well, I stopped by because . . ."

"Yes?" Mr. Keller peers at me the way he does in class when he's calling on students, like he's expecting me to say something good. I thought I'd ask for help on my land, but for some reason, I'm embarrassed. I stare through a glass panel — outside, the sun warms their yard.

"I came over because Lola's told me about your house and I wanted to see it. I'm glad I did." I smile at them. "I should get going."

"Where are you headed?" Mr. Keller asks.

"Back to the city."

"Let me give you a lift. I've got a few errands to run there."

"It's okay. I like taking the bus."

"Nonsense," Mr. Keller says, and soon we're both in his car.

■ ■ ■ ■

We cross the Golden Gate Bridge with its wide span of reddish-orange cables, our windows rolled all the way down to feel the breeze. The air on my face is cool and swift, like a poem. When I was little, I used to think the bridge was literally made from gold. It's actually painted in a color called international orange so it stands out in the fog.

This bridge always looks different. Sometimes the top's covered by thick clouds and I can't spot the city. It's like traveling into nothing, a hazy dream. It can get foggy in the summer when the ocean air rushes in and pulls the mist across. Other times, like now, it's so clear I can see across the skyline to the tip of the Transamerica Pyramid.

Today, hundreds of people line both sides, cyclers on one, walkers and joggers on the other.

"Isn't it mind-blowing, the engineering behind something as grand as this entryway? It never ceases to amaze me, but particularly on beautiful days like this," Mr. Keller says.

"Mr. K, remember how I told you I'm building my tiny house?"

"Yes, vividly."

"That's what I was doing this morning, out on my land. Mom found a new job and we might have to move out of San Francisco, so I'm building it now."

Mr. Keller watches the road and doesn't say anything right away — maybe I said too much.

"I'm sure Minda's doing what she thinks is best for your family, Lucinda. You know, my father passed away when I was around your age. Mothers usually make decisions because they're doing their best."

He's siding with her already. "How come you never had any kids?" I ask, and he laughs.

"I do have between twenty-four and twenty-eight wonderful kids of my own each and every school year. And I'm lucky to have taught for so long that I get to see a few of them grow up, too — like your mom and aunt."

I like to think of Mr. K as my substitute grandpa, and I know Lolo and Grandpa

Ted would approve. We smile at each other.

We veer off the bridge, through the tolls, and into areas of steep streets and skinny houses smushed up so close against each other that no light can squeeze through the cracks.

Lola's house sits in a pocket not far from the ocean, in a neighborhood where the homes have the teeniest of front yards. My grandparents came to San Francisco when they immigrated. The way Lola tells it, they had relatives who found them farm jobs out in the Central Valley; then during off-seasons they worked in restaurants and hotels and department stores — cleaning, fixing, serving. They worked hard to buy a place of their own, with everything they needed to raise their American daughters.

Our main street has shops and cafés and people Maribel calls "hipsters," who like to eat expensive toast, all mixed with homeless people pushing shopping carts. The opposite of Mr. Keller's quiet street.

We pull into the driveway. Mom gets home in a few hours. I suddenly think:

How am I going to explain this if Mr. Keller tells her I went to his house?

"Thanks so much, Mr. K. You don't have to walk me up."

"Oh, don't be silly," he says, and we get out of the car.

Inside, Mom's on the couch. She got home early! I walk in with Mr. Keller and she sits up, confused.

"Peter? Lou? Is everything all right?"

"Ummm . . ."

"Oh, everything's swell, Minda. We've been enjoying the beautiful weather and a nice chat. Lucinda popped by my place in Marin after she was out at her land. I think it's fabulous you let her have some independence. When I was a kid, I rode the bus everywhere on my own."

Mom still looks puzzled. "You were *where*? By *yourself*?"

"Uh . . ." I give a half-smile.

"Lucinda told me all about her little house," Mr. Keller says.

I watch her react. I'm definitely in trouble.

"Please, stay for some *merienda*. Lucinda, we'll talk about your adventure later." She's definitely mad if she's using my full first name.

"Ladies, perhaps I should bid you goodbye and be on my way to run errands."

"You're not getting off that easy, Peter. Come in. Hang out," Mom says to him.

In the kitchen, I fix myself a PB and J while they talk in the living room. I hear Mom say quietly, "She has this wacky idea to build a house out there."

"So?" Mr. Keller says. "She's very capable, Minda. That takes planning, math skills, artistic flair. . . . This would be a terrific project for her."

Mom sighs. "Oh, you woodshop people. I need Lou to get her mind on other things right now."

"What are you guys talking about?" I carry my plate into the living room.

"I was about to give you ladies something that might come in handy," Mr. Keller says. He grabs a pen and small notepad from his pocket and scribbles something, then rips out the page and hands it to me.

"My number. You already have it, but this is for your fridge, a reminder to call me anytime. You can both come over. Lou and I can do some learning while Minda and Ed catch up." He winks at me.

"That's kind of you, Peter," Mom says as she shows him to the door.

Once he's gone, she stretches out her arms. "I could use a hug." And I walk into her. She doesn't seem mad anymore.

"Sorry, Mom."

"Lou, whatever you were doing today without my permission, no more."

I nod. "May I go over to Sheryl's for a little while?"

"I was hoping to tell you all about Washington. I had a great trip," she says, smiling. Not a good sign. What if I'm already signed up for a new school?

"Sure, uh . . . that. Can we do it later?"

Mom's phone buzzes; she holds it to her ear. "Hey, sis. Yeah, just got back." She looks at me and raises a finger, asking me to wait. I hide out in the only place I can.

In my closet, on the top shelf behind stacks of books and shirts, I find Dad's dollhouse. I slide it out and set it down carefully.

He designed a Victorian — very San Francisco. Mom and I look at real ones on house tours, and I love running my hand against the wooden railings, even though you're not supposed to touch anything.

I don't play with dolls anymore, but I like to study Dad's gift. It has a slanted roof covered in rounded shingles like fish scales, and a swirly gingerbread trim. It's so detailed that if I squint, I can pretend I'm looking at something life-sized.

There's a knock at my office door.

"No one's home," I say, but Mom opens it anyway.

She squishes in and sits down, the clothes above grazing her head. "Got something for you." Mom hands me a little booklet.

I fan through pages of kids holding up

hammers and amateur birdhouses, or shovels and dirty carrots they just dug up.

"It's a group in Seattle that gives wood-working classes. They have real tools and — get this — there's a community garden you and Lola could visit."

Why would I build with those kids when I've got a project that's a trillion times better? I might as well ask. "So you liked it there?"

"I have to admit, it was pretty darn perfect. I saw some great neighborhoods and schools. . . ."

"We have those things here."

"I know, Lou, but I think you'd love it," she says, giving me her biggest smile.

"I already told you, I don't want to move."

"But you'll make good friends and have fun things to do there, too." She hesitates, then says, "Honey, there's no easy way for me to tell you this, but I've decided to take the job."

What did she just say? "Are you serious?"

"I know this isn't what you want to

hear —"

"But what about my friends? And what about our family? And Barrio Fiesta? What about my birthday . . . and my land?"

"Oh, sweetie, you'll still get to dance. We'll move after Barrio Fiesta. That gives us time to get organized, and we can celebrate your birthday here. And your land will be here whenever we visit."

"I can't believe you're doing this to me."

"Lou, you're old enough to understand this now. I've been giving the decision a lot of thought, going over all the pros and cons — this is for your future. If we stay here, we'll never be able to save for college or buy a house."

Mom tries to hug me but I snap myself away. She stays planted. We sit in silence until finally, she says, "Whenever you're ready, I'm here to talk."

Mom shuts the closet door quietly behind her.

What now?

I picture myself blowing out a candle,

and exhale slowly. My head starts to clear.

There's a tiny stairway in my dollhouse. I slide my finger down the railing, its perfect little balusters. Dad wouldn't want us to leave.

Mom's a softy when it comes to the Nelsons' land. If I stick to the original plan of building my house, I think I can still convince her not to take that job. She just needs to *see* it to understand. I'll need to build fast.

There's a picture taped to the center of my vision heart, of me and my friends on a hike in the redwoods. We're acting goofy, flexing our muscles, sipping from water-backpack tubes and trying not to laugh. I stare at it.

Okay, Lou. Step it up.

CHAPTER 11
OPERATION TINY HOUSE

Lola Day means an afternoon when Sheryl and I do different things with our grandma, like mani-pedis, even though I hate nail polish and always choose clear, or watching Lola's Filipino soap operas and making bets on what's going to happen.

But normally we do "Filipino stuff," like learning to cook new dishes or hearing about history, which means Lola makes her friends tell us stories about being in the Bataan Death March, or fighting for farmworkers with Larry Itliong and Philip Vera Cruz — they were Filipino American labor leaders. We always get good ideas for book reports.

Today is Lola Day, but mega-sized. We're taking over the community center to get ready for Barrio Fiesta.

In the kitchen, I stare into a giant stainless-steel refrigerator to find ingredients, but it's impossible to focus.

I feel an arm around my shoulders. I'd know that touch anywhere.

"Hey, Lola."

"Let us get your mind off any worries." She always seems to know when I'm feeling bad.

Expertly, Lola yanks items from the fridge and pulls me to a long table, where other *lolas* roll *lumpias.* Someone's frying them up, and the whole kitchen smells dee-lish.

Sheryl and I have a thick square stack of doughy wrappers, plus bowls of meat-and-veggie filling.

"Don't forget to wet the wrapper so it sticks at the edge." Lola dabs her finger into a bowl of water to show us — the way she always has.

Mom and Auntie Gemma have memories of doing "Filipino stuff" with Lola when they were growing up, too. Raising them in America, Lola says, she needed to teach them such things.

"Tell us again how you met Lolo," Sheryl asks. My cousin could hear that story every day and never get sick of it.

"He wooed me with a *kundiman,* a love song. It was the middle of the night, and he and his *compadres* stood outside my window strumming their guitars. But your *lolo*'s voice was so dreadful, like a squawking chicken, that all the roosters crowed and woke everyone in our village, so my father chased them away with his best machete!" She slaps her thigh and laughs hysterically. Part of why we love hearing this story is how lively she gets as she tells it. "Every single night he came back and sang me his love songs, and every single night your great-grandfather shooed him away. But one night, your great-grandpa simply invited him to come back in daylight. Lolo helped on our farm, convinced your great-grandparents of his love for me, and became a part of our family. That turned into our wonderful life."

"So romantic," Sheryl says dreamily.

"*Ay nako!* I smell something burning!" Lola says as she rushes to the stove.

Sheryl gives me a smile, but the kind she uses for poor, wounded animals at the Humane Society.

"Do the girls know yet?" she asks.

I throw a *lumpia* in the air and it lands on the table with a dull plop. I sigh.

"Nope."

"Come on, let's go tell them."

We sneak out the door and into the parking lot.

Gracie and Alexa are painting an old jeep with a mural of handprints and faces and rainbow swirls, while Annie attaches all the stuff we found at her salvage yard. The jeepney's draped with strings of bright triangle flags, the American flag, and the Philippine flag with its vibrant yellow sun. It's the most colorful ride I've ever seen.

"What do you think?" Annie asks.

"I'm not so sure. . . . It might need a bit more pizzazz," I say, and she laughs.

A pile of giant bamboo spoons coated in silver glitter paint rests at Annie's feet. We're lining the sides with them next to signs that say *Get Your Ice-Cold Halo-Halo!* and *Halo-Halo, How Are You?*

The jeepney will circle the neighborhood while selling *halo-halo,* a sweet concoction of ice, milk, red beans, tapioca pearls, jackfruit, and coconut flesh — with even sweeter condensed milk drizzled on to stir in. Yum. My favorite dessert.

The dessert-truck angle was my idea, our way to remember Lolo. He always used to tell me, *"Halo-halo* means 'mix-mix,' like you, *anak ko."*

"Get over here, Lou. I need someone who can handle a real tool," Annie says, holding up an electric screwdriver.

Annie positions a spoon on the jeep and shows me how to make adjustments before I whirl the screws in.

"Hey, Annie, when did you figure out you were good at building things?" I ask.

Mr. Keller said I remind him a little bit

of the high school version of Annie. That's the nicest compliment. She owns a successful business and has a massive collection of power tools. I'd love to turn out like her.

"Let's see. . . . I was in shop class and a boy told me, 'You build like a girl.' I knew right then that I could create anything. And what's so satisfying is that I have, just like you," she says, letting go of the spoon. "Voilà! See?" The decoration stays put.

"We did it!"

All night and morning I felt bad thinking about Mom's news, but if women like Annie have done the opposite of what people think they can do, then so can I.

"How about a break?" Annie says to the girls. "I bet the *lolas* have some good stuff for us in the kitchen."

"We'll meet you," I say.

As soon as Annie's out of sight, I tell them, "Quick! Inside the jeep!"

The four of us huddle, and I can't hold the news in any longer. "We're moving."

"What?" Alexa says.

"Oh no!" Gracie says.

They stare at me sad-faced.

"It's all good. I have a plan."

"She has a plan!" Gracie shouts, punching her fist in the air.

"And you're all involved."

"Here we go," Sheryl says.

"We're listening," Alexa says.

They lean in.

"I need help building my house. On my land. *Major* assistance. A whole crew!"

"You're going to hire a *crew*?" Gracie asks.

"Don't need to." I beam at them. "Because *you're it.*"

"What?" Alexa says, laughing. Gracie and Sheryl stare at me.

"But we're not like you, Lou," Sheryl says. "Remember in fourth grade when we made California missions and yours was from scratch and everyone else used kits from the craft store? We don't know how to build a house."

"All you have to do is follow directions. It'll be so easy, I swear."

The girls glance at each other, trying to decide whether to believe me.

"I'm also thinking that Manong Arwin could help since he likes to smash stuff, and maybe . . . Jack Allen," I say.

"Jack Allen?" Gracie says. "*You* are going to talk to Jack Allen?"

"He told me he's all into movies. I'm only going to ask him to film us," I say. "So I can put clips online."

"Good thinking," Alexa says.

"What if your mom finds out, or if she sees the videos?" Sheryl asks.

"She won't. Mom doesn't have time to look on the Internet."

"Yeah, we just have to be careful, like spies," Alexa says.

"Exactly," I say. Now they're getting it.

"Do we get to smash stuff, too?" Gracie asks.

"Absolutely."

"We're in!"

Excellent.

I face Alexa. "Since my mom's letting me spend tonight at your house, it's the perfect alibi — we'll go to my land in the morning." I turn now to Sheryl. "Can you convince Manang Maribel to drive us there without her telling your mom? Your van can hold a bunch of people. Plus, I have boxes I need to bring."

Sheryl grins. "If there's anything I'm good at, it's making my sister do stuff for me. I've got so much dirt on her."

I start to relax.

"Don't you worry, Lou. We've got your back." Gracie extends her pinky, and Sheryl and Alexa do the same. I hook mine in and we tug.

CHAPTER 12
IT'S OFFICIAL

Alexa sleeps in a four-poster bed topped with a pastel pink canopy and ruffly white edges. It's a little princessy, but still, I've always wanted a bedroom like hers — or Sheryl's or Gracie's. I can't wait to impress everyone with my own house.

We do what we always do when we hang out in her room, bicycling our legs into the drapey fabric and gossiping about boys she has crushes on. Then we talk about me for once. I tell her all about running into Jack.

"There's no way I'm letting you leave. We're building you the biggest, baddest tiny house the universe has ever seen!" she says. "You think I can get cute overalls to wear?" she adds, and I laugh.

I'm not sure how helpful Alexa will be on my crew — she hates getting sweaty — but I need her.

"I can't wait to get out there," I say with a huge grin.

She studies me. "You know why I like you, Lucinda Bulosan-Nelson? Because you have bizarre ideas that are actually sort of, kind of . . . ingenious! DIY is huge now."

We review tomorrow's plan:

She tells her mom she's going to my house.
I tell my mom I'm staying at her house.
Maribel picks us up in minivan (if Sheryl did her part).
Prep trailer bed.
Build house.

"Let's text Sheryl to see if she set up our ride," she says. I'm glad she's into it.

Alexa types: *And?*

The phone buzzes right back: *Affirmative. Proceed with Operation Tiny House.*

"Yeah! Woo-hoo! Dance party!" Alexa says, and we both jump up and wiggle on the bed, our heads knocking into the canopy. We plop down and bust up.

"Next subject. What's the deal with you and Jack Allen?" She grins and it makes me blush.

"Nothing, I told you, we just hung out."

"I think he should be your first kiss."

"Yeah, right. On what planet would Jack Allen ever like me? Regular kids at school don't even like me."

"Why do you always say that, Louie? I mean, they don't *not* like you. It's just that you confuse people when you do things like . . . convincing them to use bamboo straws instead of plastic ones because the plastic's slowly killing them with BPAs," she says, raising her arms and making a scary zombie face. Alexa cracks up. "You're always so serious about that stuff. They don't know how much fun you are."

I grab a fluffy pink pillow and cover my

head — I'm still embarrassed remembering everyone laughing at me about the straws.

"Today was a blast," she says. "I wish my family was more like yours."

"You do?"

"I wish I had a ton of cousins around. We have to fly all the way to the East Coast to see mine, and that's only every other summer."

"Want to hear something? Sometimes I get jealous of your family." I've never said this to her before.

"Let's swap!"

I love that Alexa's my good friend even though we seem different. It's like when Lola plants flowers alongside the veggies in her garden and says that even though they're opposites, they help each other grow.

"Okay. Jack. True confession?" I say.

Alexa nods vigorously.

"I like him."

She screams. We crack up.

"You girls okay in there?" her mom shouts, and we can't stop laughing. Alexa tells me more about her crushes and how she can't wait for her first kiss. We even play M-A-S-H.

Alexa writes on a sheet of paper: *Mansion, Apartment, Shack, House* — then the names of four boys: *Jack A., Mark K., Pranav S., Carver J.*

She picks a number and I draw swirls on the page until she says, "Stop!" I count the number of loops, then go from letter to letter and name to name, crossing them off until she ends up with only two: *Carver J.* and *Shack.*

Poor Alexa has to marry Carver Jamison and they'll live in a shack. We bust up some more. For my turn I change *M-A-S-H* to *M-A-S-TH* and end up with *Carver J.* and *Mansion.* "Ewwwww!" we say. I don't know which is worse — Carver or a mansion.

Alexa and I chat nonstop about my house: the TV shows that will want to interview me, the hummingbird feeders I'll hang on every tree, how I'll feel when I'm in and she can visit anytime. *"Mi casa es su casa,"* I tell her, and she says, "You better believe it."

We talk into the night — about finally

being the oldest in school, or what it might feel like to kiss a boy who likes you back, or our futures: mine as a famous San Francisco architect, and hers as a songwriter/fashion mogul/ pastry chef living in a New York loft above a cupcake store with a boyfriend who rides a moped.

Alexa's mom says through the door, "Lights out, girls."

I'm wide-awake when I should be sleeping to get ready for our big day. But I keep hearing Mom: *This is for your future.*

I poke Alexa's shoulder lightly; she doesn't budge. The clock on her desk shows that it's almost midnight.

Quietly, I wander into the family room and turn on a lamp. Maybe I can watch a little TV or read to help me fall asleep.

My phone vibrates. I look at the screen; it's not a number I know. Only a few people have my cell phone number since it's only for emergencies.

I touch the Accept circle and a square jumps out with a face in the middle. Jack's. Alexa texted him hours ago and said we needed to talk ASAP. I didn't think he'd call back.

"What's up?" he says.

"Do you have any idea what time it is?" I whisper.

"Nope."

"Midnight."

"Really?" Wherever Jack is, it's loud.

"Where are you?"

"Here." He holds up his phone for me to see — lots of kids, older ones. A face moves in so I see eyes and a nose up close. The face shouts, "Wussup, girl!"

I whisper-laugh. "Who was that?"

"No clue." Jack points the phone back to his face. "John dragged me to some high school party. Our dad's out of town, and John's supposed to be watching me. He's gonna get so in trouble when I tell on him."

"What's it like?"

"Everyone's being nice to me. I've been filming everything. They don't notice."

I slide the screen door to the porch open and tiptoe onto the back patio so I don't disturb Alexa and her parents. Now would be the perfect time to ask Jack to go with us tomorrow, but . . .

Ask him, Lou. Be bold. Say something.

"Hey, have you figured out the movie for your film-camp application?"

"Not yet."

"Do you think you'd want to film me?" I suddenly say. I didn't mean to, but I needed to get it over with.

"You?" He's surprised, but he's not laughing.

"Not me, exactly, but the work on my tiny house. We're building tomorrow. Maybe you can use the footage for your submission . . . if you wanted. A killing-two-birds-with-one-stone sort of thing."

"You want to kill birds out in the woods and have me film it?"

"No, silly, it's an expression. I help you and you help me."

"I was teasing!" He laughs. "Eighth grader builds her own house. Yeah, kinda catchy. You'd look good on camera."

"I would?" That makes me smile, but I try not to let him see.

"Sure, why not? I'll do it."

That was easy.

Jack moves his phone around so everything gets all dancey.

It's weird how I'm getting to know him. But weird-nice. It's official: my first crush.

A voice says, "Dude, come on, let's go."

Another face pops onto my screen — Jack's brother — then disappears.

"Dude, is that your girlfriend?" the voice says. The screen goes black and I can hear Jack say, "Shut up!" But the voice sings, "Jacky's got a girly-friend, Jacky's got a girly-friend. . . ." Then hyena-like laughter.

The phone cuts out.

I text him the details about tomorrow, wondering if he's still thinking about me.

CHAPTER 13
THIS IS THE BEST DAY

Gracie meets us at Alexa's and we wait out front for my cousins. They seem as excited as I feel, because we can't stop chatting. My head buzzes and my insides tingle. My whole body's letting me know: we're about to do great things.

Manang Maribel pulls up in the Filipino-Mobile, a minivan with a slew of metallic *Manila* stickers Uncle Jon-Jon slapped across the bumper. As little kids we used to love riding around in it, but now it makes us cringe.

The doors slide open and we hop in. Sheryl's in front and Arwin's in the middle. Alexa and I load in a cooler of food and drinks and a box of materials we'll need for building.

"Whoa, whoa, whoa, whoa, *whoa* . . . I didn't agree to be responsible for *all* you rug rats," Maribel says.

"We have to pick up Jack Allen, too. You know, Lou's new *love interest*?" Sheryl says. She, Alexa, and Gracie giggle. Arwin doesn't say anything, even though he knows Jack from soccer.

Maribel turns off the engine and looks at each of us.

"Please, Manang?" Sheryl says.

"Pretty please, Manang?" Alexa says.

"Por favor s'il vous plaît?" says Gracie.

Arwin plays a game on his phone.

"Remind me again what I get out of all this," Maribel says.

"Our forever gratitude?" Gracie responds.

"And?" Maribel adds.

"Uhhh . . . our blind adoration of you for life?" Alexa says.

"And?"

"And Lou and I will cover for you your whole senior year, like if you want to sneak out to parties, *and* I won't tell Mom and Dad that your Friday Night Homework Club is totally fake," Sheryl says. Maribel keeps staring. "Geez. Okay, okay already . . . and one week of Lou's allowance!"

"Wait a minute. What?" I say, and they all crack up.

Sheryl pats me on the back. "It was the only way."

Maribel gives a loud groan. "Fine. Jack, then to Lou's land. Everyone buckle up, I don't have all freaking day."

Alexa gives a little *woot!* and the minivan starts up.

At the clearing, everybody but Maribel gets out.

"You have three hours, and don't expect me to help. I'm studying for the SATs," Maribel says, wadding squishy orange plugs into her ears as she takes out a laptop and reclines in her seat.

I look around. Today we'll clean up the

trailer flatbed and get it ready to build on. Later will come wall frames, plumbing and electrical, windows, walls, and a door, and at the end, I'll lay down a beautiful wooden floor. Once it's sanded, stained, and coated, I'll slip off my socks to feel the soft texture under my feet.

"Hey, I remember this place. Wanna check out the creek?" Arwin says to Jack. They run down a slope and weave through trees before I can stop them.

"Where are you guys going?" I shout, but soon they're out of sight.

Alexa's trying to send a text (she hasn't found out yet that the reception's spotty). Gracie's trying to sit in the hammock, except she keeps flipping over and giggling. Sheryl's poking around inside the shed, and every few minutes she shouts, "Woweeeee, what is all this stuff?"

I cup my hands to my mouth and yell, "Who wants to get started?"

No one pays attention.

Jack and Arwin trudge up, barefoot, jeans rolled to their knees. "Ouch!" Arwin says, stepping on something, and Jack laughs at him.

We'll never get anything done.

You can do this, Lou. I try to morph into Mr. Keller when he's ordering everyone around in class.

"Gather round the trailer bed, folks!" I shout.

Nobody comes. I need a megaphone.

Suddenly, a piercing whistle. Maribel's got a thumb and pointer finger in her mouth, blowing loud and strong. Everyone looks at her, and Manang yells to me, "You're welcome!"

Sheryl saunters out in a bandanna, oversized goggles, a face mask, and yellow dishwashing gloves. She raises her hands and in a muffled voice says, "Full speed ahead."

"Let's do this," I tell my crew.

I take everyone to the covered trailer bed as Jack films. We stand around it, and Alexa helps me slip off the plastic tarp.

Arwin eyes it skeptically. "What's that supposed to be?"

"Is it part of an old car or something?" Gracie asks.

"It's the base for us to put the subfloor

on. Then the house," I say. I point to the metal beams. "See all these rusty areas? We have to brush that stuff off. Then we'll paint the metal so it'll look like new."

A funny thing happens, where Sheryl begins walking around the flatbed, and soon we're all following her like some kooky dance circle.

"But it seems so small for a house," Sheryl says.

"Waaaaay small," Gracie says.

"Don't you guys know anything? That's why it's called a tiny house." Arwin tries to help.

"Remember the pictures on Lou's vision heart? It'll be great," Alexa says.

After a minute, the rest of them nod, even though they still look a little doubtful.

"I'm starving. Is it snack time yet?" asks Arwin.

"We haven't even started," I say.

"Don't Auntie and Uncle ever feed you?" Sheryl asks.

"Ooooh, there's a yummy pizza place

in town. Dad and I go there after hiking," Alexa says.

I look back at Maribel in the van. She's napping.

I smile. "Guys, listen up. You all wanted in on helping, right? And I promise when we're done, this house is yours, too. Imagine having our own place," I say. "We'll have Nerf-gun parties, get a gigantic TV, and stock the kitchen with junky stuff that our moms never buy. For kids only."

They get quiet, and I show them what to do.

From the box I brought, I pull out face masks, goggles, pairs of work gloves, and metal wire brushes. Everybody gets one of each. We slide on our masks, even Jack, who makes Darth Vader noises with Arwin.

I point out smears of orangey-brown. "Find any rust and erase it."

"That's easy enough," Gracie says.

We start, getting on our knees and scrubbing in circles and lines, like brushing teeth. It's trickier than I thought. At first everyone's acting silly, but soon they start to concentrate. Even Maribel puts on gear to join us for a little while.

I stop for a second and notice: No one's talking. Everyone's brushing.

I get up to inspect.

Arwin and the others push their masks off and stretch.

"Check out these biceps. I'm getting a solid upper-arm workout," Sheryl says, flexing.

"How'd we do?" Gracie asks.

I walk around and look for any spots we might have missed, but it's clean. Practically like new.

"You did amazing! This would have taken me forever by myself."

Gracie runs to the van and brings back bottles of water that she hands out, but before they can rest, I say, "You guys are gonna love this next part."

I grab cans of spray paint. "Now we coat the beams."

Arwin slides his mask and goggles back on. "Me first!"

He shakes a can, holds it away from his

face, and aims, spraying the paint back and forth. He's doing pretty well. I put on my gear and join him.

"That's a ton of chemicals. Don't breathe any of it in," Sheryl reminds us, pulling on her face mask.

They stand back as he and I aim and spray in long, flowing lines. After we finish, I say, "Let's let it dry before the next coat."

When Arwin pulls off his gear, there's a haze of black paint outlining his eyes and nose, like a reverse raccoon. I take mine off, too, and I guess I look the same, because Arwin starts snort-laughing.

After a while the others spray on another coat, and the trailer's ready for the subfloor.

We did it. We really, truly, amazingly did it — just like I knew we would.

I hand out small reusable towels, which we soak with water to wipe our hands and faces clean. We finish up, and Arwin says, "I have a great idea!"

He sprints down the slope toward the creek, and we all follow, stopping where the stream cuts across. For a moment everyone's quiet. I dunk in my fingers, and the water shoots a delicious chill right through me.

Arwin's the first to fling off his shoes. "What are you waiting for?" he shouts.

We all do the same and wade in, ankle deep. Underneath, the pebbles feel smooth and bumpy at once.

Soon Arwin's jumping into the shallow bank as hard as he can, making huge splashes. "Don't get my camera wet, you turkey!" Jack shouts, putting his camera down near a tree. He runs to get a scoopful of water and tries to hit Arwin. Everyone's screaming and laughing.

I love that they love it out here. Still, we can't waste any time. Next step: unload wood from the shed and get it ready to measure and trim. With their help, this part should go fast.

We run back to the clearing and my neighbor Mrs. Hawkey walks up, dusting her hands on an apron covered in colorful paint drips. She's an artist. The Hawkeys are an older couple who live a few yards from here in a cabin hidden by trees. Because of them, I have even more stories of my dad. Every summer Dad and Grandpa Ted would bring sleeping bags and a guitar, and the Hawkeys would join them for late-night bonfires and s'mores.

She hugs me, Sheryl, and Maribel.

"I thought I heard some noise out here. What are you kids doing? Where are Minda and Gemma?"

I look at Maribel — so do the rest of the kids.

Manang Maribel gives Mrs. Hawkey her perfect smile. "Oh, Lou and her friends are doing a project for extra credit. I'm watching them until . . . uh . . . until Auntie Minda gets back . . . soon!"

Maribel looks at me with a face that says *I own you now.*

"I'm just a few seconds up the hill if you kids need anything," she says, and walks away with a wave as we all thank her.

The group steps back and examines our handiwork. Not bad.

"Hey, Louie, please don't kill me, but I

still don't get it. How are you going to build a house on *that*?" Alexa says.

"And it's going to be on wheels like you're going to drive it around? Is that how it works?" Gracie asks.

"Sure, my house can go anywhere I decide to take it," I say, but Sheryl stares at me. She seems doubtful. "What?" I say to her. "Spit it out."

"It's just that, well . . . . what if this *doesn't* convince your mom to stay?"

Did she really just say that? Even now I can see the whole house, inside and out: a welcome mat at the door, a red kettle on the stove, the million stars shining in through the skylight at night. If we build more, so they can see more, they'll get it, too.

"Guys, shhhhh, listen closely. Can you hear?" Arwin whispers, and we all get quiet. He lifts his shirt and squishes down on his belly, making his stomach talk to us in a deep voice: "Feeeeeeed meeeeee." The girls say, *"Grosssss!"* and Sheryl punches him hard in the shoulder.

Jack packs up his camera.

"Let's go eat," Alexa says.

"But it's not lunchtime yet. This was just a break. It's time to prep the wood," I say, but Arwin's yawning and the other kids are grabbing their stuff.

"Guys, we still have work to do!" I say.

"Geez, Louie, maybe chill out a little?" Sheryl says.

"Let's go, little humans. Time's up," Manang Maribel says, and they jump back into the Filipino-Mobile.

CHAPTER 14
JUST KEEP BUILDING

Tonight's our family dim sum dinner at Lola's favorite Chinese place. She says that even our rice cooker needs a night off every now and then. Sheryl's family and Lola are already at the restaurant.

Mom and I get off the bus in China-town and stroll down a packed street. It's still light out.

Puffy red lanterns hang high between buildings, strung like beads on a neck-lace. Trinkets in large baskets line the sidewalks, and stores show off rows of yummy things like savory buns and whole fried ducks.

I'm amazed at how much we got done today. We'll finish the house in no time. Mom will see, and we'll stay put. A smile stretches across my face.

"Did you have a good day?" I ask Mom. She seems surprised at my question.

"I did. I went to visit one of the Oakland hospitals I interviewed with."

I freeze. People around us keep walking.

"You're not taking the job in Washington?"

"Well, Oakland General hasn't made me an offer — not yet. But it seems like they're interested, so I went to find out more about their benefits. Unfortunately, they don't pay as much. My decision hasn't changed, honey. The Washington hospital is still our best choice in the long run."

Mom looks at me with concern, but I don't get upset. "That's too bad." She studies me as we keep walking.

"What about you and Alexa? What did

you girls do today?"

"We just hung out," I say cheerfully.

I pause at a storefront full of tchotchkes. We love looking in the Chinatown shops at all the fun knickknacks. She picks up a small grinning Buddha and rubs its round belly.

"You know, Lou, we haven't really talked since the other day, but I'm so glad to see you're feeling better about everything." She smiles at me like she thinks I've accepted her decision.

I pick up a ceramic fortune cookie with a slip of paper sticking out: *Your strength is your own belief.*

"Much better," I say, because my house is on its way.

Mom sits with our family at two huge round tables. Dim sum ladies wheel silver carts of small platters up to them, and everyone points to what they want.

I find my cousins at their normal spot, around the lobster tank, where Sheryl taps on the glass. We watch the creatures crawl over each other. A lobster's home is its shell, which it sheds to grow. How can I leave my tiny house when I haven't had the chance to grow into it yet?

After family dinner Lola and I hang out in her favorite spot: her backyard. She uses clippers and expertly snaps at leaves and branches.

My grandma's garden feels like a wonderland, with trees full of bright lemons and limes, and large wooden planters overrun with leafy greens and all kinds of herbs. I rub a sprig of rosemary and bring its clean, strong scent to my nose the way she taught me.

Lolo and I built these planters — my first time using a handsaw. Lola said I was too young, but Lolo said not to worry since in the Philippines I'd be tending the farm, so what was the harm? We filled them with dark soil, deep and cool. He let me sink my hands and feet in.

Lola brought out a tray of *halo-halo* to celebrate the finished product. Our spoons clinked in the glasses as we mixed up the ice, and Lolo told me about his farming days in the Philippines. During dry seasons they planted tobacco and in wet months, rice.

"But these planters won't be for tobacco," Lola said that day. "We will grow beans and squash and *kamote.*" Sweet potato. "This is not the right climate for *kamote,* but we will still try. That's our only job, *anak,* simply to try."

My whole life I've watched Lola work this garden with her small but strong hands. When they first came to California, my grandparents picked asparagus in the spring and grapes in the summer and fall. For days at a time they'd leave my mom and auntie with relatives so they could travel for work.

It used to upset me hearing stories of how people treated them because of their dark skin and thick accents — until Lola taught me that everyone has a history and theirs gave us our good life now. "That's how sacrifice works."

Now Lola takes a break from clipping bushes and reclines in a lawn chair, tilting her face toward the sky. It's getting darker, a dreamy nightfall-gray.

I wish she could fix how mixed-up I feel.

"Lola, do you remember how you

promised to help me grow a garden in front of my tiny house?" It was her suggestion. "How will we do that if Mom and I don't live near you anymore?"

I take my phone and show her pictures of the trailer bed all cleaned up. She squints and pushes the screen away.

"Anak ko," she says. She claps her hands in a rhythm and sings:

"Bahay kubo, kahit munti.
Ang halaman doon, ay sari-sari.
Sinkamas at talong, sigarilyas at mani.
Sitaw, bataw, patani."

"Ay nako! My voice used to be prettier," she says, laughing. "Do you remember that song?"

She's always sung it to us. It reminds me of nights I loved, Lola and Mom singing me to sleep together. They would try to harmonize but always sounded kind of awful. Mom would laugh and laugh.

Nipa hut — even though it is small,
The plants that grow around it are
    varied.
Turnip and eggplant, winged bean

153

and peanut,
String bean, hyacinth bean, lima bean.

"When I was a girl, my wish was to get far away from the *bahay kubo.* I wanted to give my family more. And now look at you, bringing the one-room house back into style," she says, chuckling.

"I don't want to move."

"I don't want you to, either, but your mama's working hard to give you the same thing I wanted for my daughters — a better life. You will both figure it out."

I wish I could feel the same.

The doorbell rings and I open it to find a person in a brown uniform.

"Delivery for Luzviminda Bulosan."

Mom zips over. He hands her a large envelope and an electronic clipboard to sign. The envelope looks official.

"What'd you get?" I ask as she shuts the door.

Mom opens the package and pulls out a sheet of paper. I watch her eyes move, reading it. "Oh my."

"What happened?"

She covers her face with her hands for a second.

Lola walks in. "Who was there?"

My mother looks at me. "Lou, honey, we need to talk."

Mom and I sit down in the dining room, the letter resting on the table in front of us.

"It's from the county," Mom says. "A notice of public auction."

"What does that mean?" Lola asks, taking a seat.

Mom picks up the letter and stares at it for a long moment. "This has to do with Lou's land. If the taxes aren't paid on time, then after a certain number of years, the county has the right to auction it off."

"I don't get it," I say.

"Lou, the county's going to sell your land if we don't pay them more money."

"What?" Am I really hearing this? I look from Lola to Mom.

Lola leans forward. "How much more do you owe, *anak ko*? I thought you had gotten things under control?"

"I worked out a settlement plan a while back, but between the taxes and late fees and paying for school . . . it's been impossible to keep up."

"Is this the first time they've contacted you about this?" Lola asks.

Mom shakes her head. "No."

Her face wrinkles and she begins to cry. I feel numb.

"Is there anything we can do?" Lola asks calmly.

Mom wipes her eyes and scans the letter again. She reads it aloud, slowly. " 'We have the right to redeem the property by the close of business on the last business day prior to the sale. . . . The auction is planned for twenty-one days from now.' " She grabs her phone and looks at the calendar. "That means we have until the Monday after Barrio Fiesta to pay everything off."

"Are you kidding me?" I say. I can feel my hands trembling.

"There is still time. We will figure out what to do," Lola says, though she looks worried, too.

My mind races as I try to understand. "I'm still building my house. I just went out there today. If I finish, maybe the county won't go through with the auction if they see a structure there."

"Your house?" Mom looks at me, still shocked. "Lou, have you been going out there again on your own?"

"I wasn't alone. I had helpers. What else am I supposed to do?"

"Lou. You are grounded. No trips to the land." Mom sighs, then shakes her head. "Let's all calm down and try to think logically," she says. "With my new job I'll get a big raise — so between that and what I've been saving, I'll pay what I can, then arrange another payment schedule. They allow people to do that."

I jump up. "Are you sure that's going to work?"

"I can help, too." Lola takes Mom's hand.

"You already have, but somehow I still got us to this point."

"I wish you had told me sooner, Minda," Lola says.

"I didn't want to burden anyone,"

Mom says.

"Is there anything else we can do right away?" I ask, but they start talking to each other, leaving me out. "Mom?"

She looks into my eyes. "Lola's right, honey. We'll figure this out. *I'll* fix this."

"How could you let this happen?" I yell before running into my closet and slamming the door as hard as I can.

I'll have to figure this out myself. On my phone, I search for *taxes and land*. A bunch of legal stuff pops up, and I'm not sure what any of it means. My head throbs. It's too hard to think.

Okay. Breathe.

If the county wants to sell . . . I know! I'll chain myself to my land! People did that in Berkeley when the city wanted to cut down a hundred-year-old tree. My friends can come, and when the tax collectors see us, they'll be so confused they'll leave it alone!

No, no, no. Dumb, dumb, dumb idea.

Or maybe if I keep building, they can't hold the auction if there's already a house on the land? But it's on wheels — they'd tell us to drive it away.

That won't work, either.

I wish I could just keep building and not have to worry about this. I stare at my new screen saver — a picture of me in front of that tiny house I visited. If only it were my house.

My house.

That's it! I know what I can do!

I dig into my jeans pocket and the slip of paper's still there. I dial the number scrawled on it, and a voice answers.

"Mr. Keller? It's Lou. I need your help, please. Big-time."

Sheryl, Gracie, and I sit at our favorite corner boba tea shop. It's right down the block from Lola's, which is the only reason our parents let us come here by ourselves.

Gracie sips from her straw and tries to slurp up a boba ball as slowly as she can. We watch the dark, round gummy inch up — then shoot into her mouth. Gracie looks surprised and Sheryl laughs.

I've told them my new plan: Build the

house, then sell the house.

"Mom's going to come up with the money and I'm going to help her. But it means I have to build faster. Lightning speed," I say.

"I thought it was supposed to be *our* house," Gracie says. "All that work just to sell it?"

"We can't have a house if I don't have a place to put it. If I'm going to save my land, I have to *get doing,*" I say. "It's fine. It's good practice so I can build again later. Lolo used to say practice makes perfect. The most important thing now is getting the money, and people buy those premade ones for thousands and thousands of dollars. I checked online — it's true!"

"My dad said the Bay Area's the most expensive place in the country for real estate, and since there's not a lot of choices, some people will shell out anything for a house, even million-dollar fixer-uppers. He says they're idiots. So I bet you could do it," Gracie says.

"How are you going to get out there if you're grounded?" Sheryl asks.

"Mom said I could, because Mr. K's

helping me today."

Mom got mad after I let it slip out that I went to the land again. But when I asked her if I could spend today with Mr. Keller learning stuff, she seemed happy to say yes — I think she felt bad about the auction letter. I just left out the part about working on my house (whoops).

"I wish we could go with you," Gracie says.

"No sweat."

We lean our heads forward to sip our drinks, lines of boba balls marching up the straws. The girls have other things they're doing today, but I don't mind. I'm going to have a real expert to help me build.

Chapter 15
Not Like the Others

A car honks. I run outside as Mr. Keller rolls up to the house in a flashy red pickup.

"Whoa, cool ride!"

He pats the dashboard. "You like?"

When I called Mr. Keller, I asked, "Can you help me build my house?"

He jumped right in with questions about what plans I made or tools I had, then said, "How about we survey things together, if your mom's okay with that?"

I hop into Mr. Keller's truck.

"One quick pit stop," he says.

We drive into Annie's Salvage Yard, and when Annie sees us, she walks out carrying a large toolbox. "Why, it's my two favorite builders." She puts the box in the truck bed.

"What are we doing here?" I ask.

"You'll need the proper tools, right? We'll bring some with us," Mr. Keller says.

Fernando carries out a framing nailer and an orbital sander and other tools with gears and handles and sharp edges.

"But I don't have the money for any of these," I say.

"It's all right," Annie says. "This stuff's just been sitting around. Think of them as borrowed. We'll lug 'em back here once your project's finished."

"Oh, Annie, you're the best," I say, giving her a hug. "Can you come with us?"

"I thought you'd never ask. I'll join y'all after I finish up in the office."

■ ■ ■ ■

I invited Jack to film again and he surprised me by saying yes, but I didn't tell him who'd pick us up. He climbs into the back of Mr. Keller's truck with a tripod. I think Jack's a little scared of our teacher; he doesn't say much.

Mr. Keller points his nub at him. "Pull my finger."

Jack looks horrified. Mr. Keller and I crack up.

"Hardy har har," Jack says.

At the clearing, we all get out. Truck doors slam and birds high up in treetops scatter in all directions. Mr. Keller gazes around. "What a wondrous place."

Not long after, Annie drives up and jumps out. "Lou, I can't believe this. It's like a storybook out here."

Yes! They see it, too.

I introduce Annie to Jack and she smiles at him. "I've heard some very nice things about you, Mr. Jack Allen."

I'm too embarrassed to look his way. I don't want Jack to think I talk about him (even though I do), but he doesn't seem to notice, because he whips out a camera and points it at me. I block my face. Without the other kids, I'm shy.

"This was your idea, remember?" he says.

"I know." My dumb bright idea.

"Just act natural. Pretend I'm not here."

"Give us the grand tour," Mr. Keller says.

With Jack filming, I show them what's in the shed, the trailer bed, and finally, my blueprint. I unroll it across the hood of Mr. Keller's truck and he peers in close. I'm not a mathlete, but I had to figure out a lot of measurements.

"How'd I do?"

"You designed this all on your own?" He's still studying it.

"Just me and the Internet."

"Oh my, Lucinda, I am impressed! I've always known you could achieve big things." Mr. Keller beams at me. "You'll build this house, no problem. Piece of cake!" He pats me on the shoulder and Jack smiles. "I must be a pretty stellar teacher, huh?"

He makes me feel so good, I start laughing.

"The best!" I *can* do this.

"Okay, what's next?" Annie rubs her hands together.

"I thought we could measure and cut some wood," I say.

"First things first," Mr. Keller says. He sprints to his truck and brings back a boxy black radio with speakers. "I'm not sure your generation knows what this is, but let's give it a shot."

"Is that a boom box?" Jack takes the camera away from his face. "My dad has one. He puts it on his shoulder and dances around, which is something I can never un-see."

Our teacher slips in a cassette tape and presses a button. The music is some kind of oldies rock 'n' roll that Lola might boogie to while gardening.

He points to the open shed. "Shall we?"

Annie, Mr. Keller, and I unpack every-thing from his truck. I pull out a box of metal brackets, nuts and bolts, drill bits and nails — things that clank together as I set it down. We lift out a table with metal beams. "Is this a saw stand?" I ask.

He nods. "For the miter saw. I brought a generator, too, so we can get power to these tools. Given any thought yet to electricity for your house?"

"Solar," I say firmly, though I don't know much about it. He and Annie can teach me.

"Woodpile time," I say, and we begin moving bundles out of the shed.

Jack blends into the background, but I'm happy he's here.

"Who's used a chop saw?" Mr. Keller asks. I shoot up my hand.

He demonstrates how to use the machine safely, then asks, "Ready?"

I slide on goggles and noise cancelers. With his help, I set down a plank. The saw screeches, and slowly, I pull down until the sharp teeth meet wood. It slices right through. My first cut!

After a few more we take a break. "This land is a lovely legacy for you, Lucinda," Mr. Keller says. "When your mom and

Michael started dating, the first thing she told me was that he was a builder. Your father would have loved this."

It feels nice to talk about Dad here. If he were alive, days like this would be our Ultimate Saturdays.

We lay wood onto the trailer bed like a puzzle, and I pound a nail into a plank. There's something soothing about the steady beat of a hammer, and I start to calm. I'm going to finish this house and stop that auction.

Finally, after what feels like a very long day, we have the skeleton of a floor. I give everyone a huge grin as we clean up.

Jack aims the camera at my new sub-floor. "Tell me what this is."

I shout, "Freedom!" I laugh. "My dream project."

"Where'd you learn how to build like this?"

"From school, from my favorite teacher, and from the Internet. And books. Do you read books, Jack?" I ask, trying to make a joke, but he doesn't laugh.

He only says, "I've never met a girl like

you before."

"A girl like what?"

He shrugs. "A girl not like the others."

Is that good or bad? I'm flustered, but say, "I'll take that as a compliment."

Jack's seeing me with huge sweat stains under my armpits and messy hair and all smelly, but I don't care, because it feels like I can do anything now. Finish building by Barrio Fiesta? What Mr. Keller said: *Piece of cake.*

CHAPTER 16
WE BARELY STARTED

"All right, dancers, less than three weeks till showtime," Miss Jovy says. Today we practice in small groups, and mine's the last to go. "Lou's group, you're up!"

"You mean Team Trip?" one of the kids says, and they snicker. It's because I keep flubbing. I'm too distracted. I got so much done with Mr. Keller and Annie on the house, but I haven't gone out there since last week — the clock's ticking.

The pole holders kneel onstage and

grip their bamboo.

The music starts. The reeds clap. I hop in . . . but miss the beat, and my ankle catches. The whole group stops. Sheryl's laughter travels from the audience to the stage, and I stick my tongue out at her.

Miss Jovy sighs. "Again, please."

The music starts, the poles clap, but déjà vu. I trip.

My goof-up starts a chain reaction. Cody trips, one of the pole guys misses his beat, and we're all out of sync.

"Goodness gracious, it's time for a break. Be back in ten," Miss Jovy says, throwing her arms up. The kids all cheer and run off.

Sheryl and Gracie meet me. "Let's get a snack," Gracie says.

We head next door to the Asian grocery store for a bag of shrimp chips to share — delicious, crispy, salty, French fry-looking crackers that make my mouth pucker. In the parking lot we toss chips in the air and try to catch them in our mouths.

"I told my cousins about you. They.

Are. *Impressed.* They said you sound super smart. I invited them over when the house is finished," Gracie says happily.

"Good, because the floor looks real now. I made huge progress out there with Annie and Mr. Keller."

"How much more time do you have?" Sheryl asks.

"Until Barrio Fiesta." Hearing me say this makes them take a big breath.

"That's it?" Gracie says. "That's only a few more weeks, Lou."

"You don't think I can do it?"

"It's not that you can't, Louie, but, well . . . it's a lot of effort for something you're not sure about," Sheryl says. "And if you do finish, how do you know you can sell it? That takes a lot of work, too. You're almost out of time."

Sheryl always has to think of every worst thing that could happen.

"What other options do I have? We're not rich. Mom's still trying to figure out how to pay them."

"Geez, Lou, you don't have to get so

upset. I'm just trying to help," Sheryl says.

"If you want to help, then you can come out there with me again tomorrow," I say, but the girls stay quiet. "Gracie?"

"Lou, maybe Sheryl's on to something."

"But I have to at least try, right? Please? With the three of us there, I'll get a lot more done. You're my last hope."

Whenever Gracie's deciding on something, I can see it on her face. Her eyes glance from the empty bag of chips to the sky and finally back to me. The doubt on her face disappears.

"Okay, if you think this can work, it will," Gracie says. "We won't let you down. We'll tell our moms they scheduled an extra dance practice." I knew I could count on her.

"I thought you were coming to my house tomorrow?" Sheryl says to Gracie.

"Yeah, but Louie needs us."

Sheryl frowns at Gracie. "I'm really sorry, Lou, but . . . I'm sort of busy."

"With what?"

"With . . . chores."

"I can help you finish them after," I say.

"It doesn't matter. Maribel won't drive you. She said so."

Why's she making me feel like I did something wrong? "Are you mad at me?" I ask.

"No, I just don't feel like going. I have my own things to do."

Gracie says, "Oh, come on, Sheryl, it'll be fun. We'll take the bus like Lou and Alexa do. I've never ridden one without my parents, and it's on my bucket list."

She gives Sheryl a begging look. Rather than listen to me, my cousin listens to her. "Fine, I'll help."

I sit with Gracie and Sheryl on the bus, none of us saying much. I'm feeling better; with the three of us building today, it'll go fast. Then Sheryl says, "Maybe we shouldn't be doing this, Lou. We're not allowed out there."

"Too late now," Gracie says.

"Trust me," I say, but Sheryl only stares out the window.

After getting dropped off on the main strip, we walk up to the clearing.

Gracie says, "It's chilly."

None of us brought jackets and we're wearing shorts and tees. I thought it'd get sunnier once we crossed the bridge, but the weather's overcast, a dull gray.

We set our backpacks down. Sheryl peers around. "It's kind of creepy right now."

"And freezing. My fingers are like icicles." Gracie rubs her hands.

"It'll warm up once we get moving." I try to sound cheery. I search the shed for work gloves. "We'll trim more wood, then start turning it into the walls. Help me move the planks out."

I toss them each a pair of gloves and we slip them on.

"Let's do it," I say.

Sheryl lifts one end of a stack and Gracie takes the other. They drag it outside but let go. Dirt and leaves puff up.

"Guys, be careful," I say.

"This is way too heavy," Sheryl says.

We try again. This time I take one end of a bundle and Sheryl lifts the other. We manage to walk it out, slowly, and lower it to the tarp. The three of us take turns moving wood, and soon we're breathing hard.

Sheryl folds her arms. "You want us to do this all day?"

"Are you here to help me or not?"

Drizzle floats over the hilltop and the sky gets cloudier.

"It's kind of weird, Louie, not having anyone else with us." Gracie looks around. "It feels too deserted; I think I want to go now."

"But we just started."

"I knew I shouldn't have let you talk me into this," Sheryl says.

"What's your problem?"

"My problem is you're so bossy. All you do is boss us around, and you've barely said thank you. You don't even know for sure if this will stop the auction."

Sheryl yanks her gloves off and throws them onto the ground.

"Sorry, Louie." Gracie pulls her gloves

off. "You should tell your mom. Maybe she found enough money and you can quit now."

I gawk at them. They're abandoning me? They're supposed to be my friends.

"My mom doesn't understand any of this, and you know what? Neither do you. You have dads and sisters and bedrooms. You have everything I'll never have."

They look kind of shocked, but they know it's true.

I try to lift a plank. "Gracie, grab the other end." She just stands there.

"I'm done," Sheryl says.

"It's not time to go yet," I say.

Sheryl slings on her backpack. "Come on, Gracie."

"Fine. You know what? I don't need you. I can do this myself."

I bend down to get a good grip on the wood and hoist the plank onto my shoulder. I imagine the Filipino villagers moving a heavy *bahay kubo* like this, with no other choice.

I swing around and almost hit Sheryl. She ducks and I drop the plank. She's fallen; the wood's on top of her foot.

"Oh no! Are you all right?" Gracie and I help her up.

"We're outta here," Sheryl says, but as she tries to walk she lets out a little yell.

"What is it?" Gracie asks.

Sheryl takes a step but then winces and lowers herself to the ground.

"Can you walk?" Gracie asks. Sheryl shakes her head.

"Are you sure? Can you stand?" I ask, but she starts to cry. Gracie looks at me.

"I'll be right back," I say, running up to Mrs. Hawkey's as fast as I can. I bang on the door. No answer.

What should I do?

I dial Mom's number but can't get a signal. I wave my phone around and try different spots in the yard until finally, a connection.

"Mom, Sheryl's hurt. Can you come right away?"

We sit and wait for Mom on a cold, damp tarp. Sheryl has stopped crying, but her toe is bruised and swelling up. She won't talk to me. No one's talking.

Mom finally drives into the clearing and runs out to examine Sheryl's foot.

"Let's help you into the car," Mom says.

Sheryl sits in the front with her foot propped up and an ice pack on it.

How could this have happened? I'm shaking.

We speed past hills and shoot through the tunnel that launches us back into the city. As soon as we reach the other end, cars line the road. Traffic. Tons.

I think about reaching over Mom and honking the horn. I just want to get Sheryl to the doctor.

It's drizzling out. Mom turns on the wipers and they make a smeary film.

"What were you girls doing out there? Lucinda? Do you have an explanation?"

"I'm sorry," I say.

Mom grips the steering wheel in tight fists. "Your cousin got hurt, and you're lucky it wasn't anything much worse."

"I know! I'm really, really sorry."

"It was an accident, Auntie," Gracie says.

Sheryl just glares out the window. Gracie does, too.

Finally, the traffic clears and our car moves. For the rest of the ride it's silent inside, drizzly outside. Mom keeps her eyes on the road. I wonder if she ever thinks about my dad dying in a car crash on the freeway. Sometimes I do.

We drop Gracie off, then Sheryl.

"I'll help you in," I say to Sheryl, but she says, "Don't."

Mom takes Sheryl up to the house and speaks to Auntie Gemma at the door before coming back to the car.

For the last few minutes, it's easiest not to talk. Finally, we inch into the driveway. The engine stops and Mom stares at me.

"What's gotten into you, Lucinda?"

"You're moving us away and I'm losing my land . . . and you're asking *me* that?"

"Do not use that tone," she says. "Whatever you girls were doing out there, you're not allowed back anymore — not by yourself, not with Mr. Keller,

180

not with anyone. Do you understand? We'll talk about your consequence later. Now please go to your room."

"My room? What room?"

I slam the car door and run down the street, my speed picking up as the road slopes down, blocks and blocks, straight to the ocean. She runs after me, then stops.

It's dusk at the beach, and the drizzle has cleared. Couples make out and surfers on the water bob up and down like buoys, waiting for waves. They're all wearing thick wet suits.

I slip off my shoes and walk the ocean's edge, the way I used to with Lolo. He'd swing me like a pendulum while the water lapped at our ankles. Water always soothes me: hearing its movement, swimming in it, or watching the waves tumble. As a toddler, whenever I had tantrums, Mom would run a warm bath and dunk me in, and I'd calm down.

The foam rolls back and I step in. My bare foot makes an impression in the sand.

"Spot me a ciggie?" a homeless lady

asks, and I shake my head. Instead, I reach into my pocket and fish out everything I have. I hand her the few bills and she says, "God bless you."

Sheryl's hurt because of me. She was right; I've taken my friends for granted. Sometimes I forget to say thank you or — my mom's favorite — "I appreciate you." I shouldn't push my friends or family. This dream belongs to only me.

The hairs on my arms stick straight up. I rub the goose bumps and turn toward home.

CHAPTER 17
SOMETHING TO
KNOW YOU BY

I'm in bed but wide-awake. Through the wall I hear someone crying. I look over at Mom's side of the room and she's not there.

The door to my grandma's bedroom is slightly open, so I poke my head in. Mom and Lola sit on the bed. Lola's arm is around Mom. My grandma might look skinny and frail, but I know her grip is strong. It comforts.

The room is simple: clean, no clutter.

A rosary of dark wooden beads hangs on a wall. On the nightstand is an old photo of our big happy family at Christmastime. Lolo wears a fuzzy Santa hat and Lola has on reindeer antlers and a spongy red nose — he's kissing her cheek. Grandpa Ted's in this one, too, with me sitting high atop his shoulders and huge grins on our faces.

Next to the pictures stand tall glasses of candles painted with intricate images of golden crosses and the Virgin Mary. Sheryl and I call this Lola's Jesus table, and we used to dare each other to stare at the scarily realistic art.

They notice me at the doorway.

"You're still awake, *anak ko*? Come, come sit with us," Lola says. "Your mama and I are having a nice talk."

"Is everything okay?" I ask.

Mom's eyes are puffy from crying. She wipes her face and waves me over, but I don't budge. She tries to smile at me.

"I was just telling your *lola* that Oakland General offered me the job."

"They did? We're staying?"

"I wish it were that simple, honey,"

Mom says. "I haven't changed my mind. The Washington job is still the better offer."

"What about the auction?" I ask.

"Lou, I'm doing everything I can to keep your land. I always have. I'm scheduling a meeting with the county to see what we can do. We'll take it from there."

"When's the meeting? Can I go?"

"It's probably best if not," she says. "I should hear back from their office soon about a date."

Mom works so hard — going back to school, putting in extra hours. If we didn't have my land anymore, maybe she wouldn't have to struggle so much. But I can't imagine letting it go.

"Instead of worrying, why don't you both join me in a prayer?" Lola says.

She's always trying to get us to go to Mass every Sunday, but Mom likes to remind Lola that even the Pope says you don't have to go to church to pray, that finding peace in nature can act as church, too.

"Oh, Mom," she says.

"You know, Minda, praying can simply

be thinking and hoping."

Lola strikes a match and lights the candles. Mom kneels beside her and they clasp their hands. I stay planted.

"Go ahead, Minda."

Mom closes her eyes, but it takes her a long time to say anything. I'm about to leave them alone when I hear her say, "I want to make progress and keep working hard for our family. For Lou." Mom's voice sounds firmer now.

With their heads bowed and eyes shut, Lola and Mom stay in their own thoughts. The candles on the nightstand flicker and I slip back into our bedroom.

If I can't build anymore, then it's time for a different plan.

I wonder where she put that auction letter?

Mom keeps all her important stuff locked in a filing cabinet: her passport, my birth certificate, her engagement ring from Dad, which she lets me try on. Sometimes she wears it around her neck on a chain, the diamond dropping low enough to touch her heart.

I grab the key from under her mattress and unlock the drawer. Inside, there's a stack of documents held together by a paper clip. I flip through it.

The auction letter is on top, and under it are a notice of sale of tax-defaulted property, a notice to parties of interest, redemption amounts, rights of parties of interest after sale . . .

I find what I'm looking for: *County Tax Collector.*

I memorize the collector's name and put the papers back where I found them.

A little red box with swirly golden borders peeks out of the cabinet. I open it — the necklace chain's there, but the engagement ring is gone.

Someone's footsteps near, so I lock the drawer quick.

I shut myself in the closet to get eye level with my giant heart. Looking at the pictures always makes me feel better.

There are some from my parents' college days — Michael and Minda — M & M. The one I love most shows them with a skyline of hills and the Golden

Gate Bridge in the background, looking so happy. She's pregnant, his hand resting on her basketball belly. He's gazing at her.

I know my dad's face, but I wish I knew his voice. If I had a genie's lamp, I'd wish to hear him, just once. Mom says that Dad and Grandpa Ted had the same kind of warm tone, low and soft, good for storytelling.

There's a picture of Grandpa Ted and me wearing matching flannel shirts, getting ready to hike. I remember that day. We walked a long trail and he told me about Dad's hobbies at my age: building the most complicated Erector sets, folding paper airplanes to get the tail just right, and drawing pictures of pretend cities — the same things I loved to do.

I know Mom's trying her best, but I'm the last Nelson, the only one who can save that land now.

I flip open our laptop and search the name until I find an official-looking site. In a few clicks I finally land on *Roger Rodrigo, County Tax Collector.*

There's a number. I grab my phone and dial.

"Please call back during normal business hours."

What do I need to make this happen?

I glance around as if I'll magically find the answer in my closet. . . . My eyes meet the vision heart. And just like that, I do.

CHAPTER 18
NEXT-BEST THING

We had a long night full of worries and tears, but the sun always rises — and I came up with a brilliant new plan.

I sit at the kitchen table and watch Mom making coffee in her fluffy white bathrobe. Coffee tastes gross, but I love the smell of it brewing.

"Oh, Lou, sweetheart." Mom pours herself a cup. She grabs a glass of OJ and slides it to me. "I'm sorry for everything."

Mom doesn't seem mad anymore for what happened to Sheryl, just tired. She takes a long, slow sip.

"How's Manang doing?" I ask. "Did you hear from Auntie yet?"

"She's better. She fractured her toe."

I feel so awful. Sheryl's going to hate me forever. "Do you think she'll still talk to me?"

Mom pats my hand. "Why don't you go talk to her? You have that secret cousin bond. Let her know how terrible you feel and that you're sorry."

I nod.

"I have to get ready for my shift, but Auntie's dropping you off at the senior center. Dance practice today *only.* Understood?"

That's exactly what I'm counting on.

I'm back in the closet with our laptop, putting the final touches on my next plan, when the doorbell rings and I hear Lola say, "Lou? You have a visitor. . . ."

What now?

In our living room, hands shoved into his pockets and peering around, is Jack Allen.

I feel my face flush — not because of the giant bamboo utensils and huge painting of Jesus's Last Supper hanging in the dining room, but because Lola's grinning at him.

"Would you like something to eat, young man?" Lola asks.

I knew she was going to say that.

"No, thank you."

"Are you sure? I made some *bibingka*. It's a sweet rice cake, Lucinda's favorite," she says, although with her accent it sounds like "pay-bor-it." "I'll go get some, okay?" She flashes him a smile and goes into the kitchen.

"Sorry, my grandma's that way to everyone."

"It's cool. I don't even have a grandma."

"What are you doing here?"

Jack holds out a small plastic memory stick. "I edited some videos you can use."

He came all this way for that?

"Gosh, thank you. It's perfect timing. I'm putting together something important, and I could use some clips."

"Did you hear any news from Mr. K about that contest yet?" he asks.

"What contest?"

Lola carries in a tray of rice cakes wrapped in banana leaves and two glasses of milk. "You eat, you eat now, okay?" she says to Jack.

"Oh, no thank you, my dad's waiting outside in the car. But I'll take one to go. Thanks!"

"Let me invite your father in," Lola says. With my back to Jack, I beg her with a look to stop, but he grabs a rice cake and hurries out. "You come visit another time, young man!"

I peek through the window — he spots me and waves. Shyly, I wave back.

Did Jack Allen just give me a gift? There's one person who'll definitely want to hear this.

"May I please go to Sheryl's now to see how she's doing?" I hold the memory stick Jack gave me — I can't wait to see what he made. Hopefully Sheryl's not upset anymore so she can watch the videos with me.

"Okay, but you eat first," Lola says, shoving the milk and dessert in my direction. I unpeel the sticky leaf and bite into its sweetness.

When I walk into my cousin's house, Auntie Gemma's in the kitchen doing a million things at once. The women in our family always look that way.

"Hey, you," she says. I was scared she'd be mad, but Auntie's smiling. "Help me out?" She nods toward the sink. "Rice."

As a little kid, one of the first things I ever learned to do with my hands was the ritual of rice — washing it, cooking it. It's the main side dish in our house for all three meals. I remember my first sleepover at Alexa's. For breakfast we had waffles and bacon and eggs, and her mom looked at me curiously when I said, "But where's the rice?"

I scoop grains from a bag and pour them into a silver container. They whoosh in and it sounds like rain. Next I turn on the tap until the water skims the grains. That's my signal to dip in. I pull and swirl the granules with my fingers and the liquid goes milky; rinse and repeat until the water goes clear.

When I'm finished, I dry my hands and Auntie wraps a hug around me. She kisses my forehead.

"How's Manang doing?" I ask.

"She's a little upset that she can't perform, but she'll be fine. This is what your *lolo* would have called a lesson in resilience."

Sheryl's had to practice so much to get over feeling anxious. After all that hard work, I'd feel bummed, too.

"She wouldn't have gotten hurt if it wasn't for me lying, Auntie. I'm sorry."

"Your *manang*'s in her room. I'm sure she'd like to see you."

I knock on Sheryl's door. "It's me. Can I come in?"

"Go away."

"Please?"

It's quiet until finally she says, "Whatever."

Sheryl sits in bed with her foot propped up.

"How are you feeling?"

"How do you think I'm feeling?" She grabs her hamburger pillow and clutches it.

"I'm sorry about everything, Manang. And I'm sorry you can't dance in the show."

She pauses, then throws the hamburger

at me. "I'm kind of relieved. But don't tell Mom or Maribel." She looks at me and her frown turns into a smile. Thank goodness.

I sit with her on the bed. "Does it hurt?"

"Not as much. I just have a little limp."

"I shouldn't have forced you to go out there. I got mad because I thought you were abandoning me."

"I'm sorry, too. I don't know what happened. I think I got jealous of all the attention you were getting. . . . And then you said that thing about not having anyone — no sisters — remember? Maribel and I think of you as our sister. We always have, so that hurt."

"I'm lucky," I say, putting my arm around her. As an only child I might get lonely sometimes, but cousins are the best.

"Did your mom freak out?"

"Oh yeah. I'm even more grounded now. Probably through the entire eighth grade."

"Sorry, Lou."

"But can I tell you my new idea?"

She gives me her uh-oh look. Someone knocks.

"It's not locked," Sheryl says, and Auntie pokes her head in.

"I'm dropping Lou off, unless you want to go hang out, maybe help with some of the final touches onstage? I already told Miss Jovy you won't be dancing."

"Oh, I hate it so much that I can't perform," Sheryl says, and I try not to laugh.

Into my ear she whispers, "Tell me your idea when we get there."

The auditorium has the energy of a popcorn machine. Dancers spin onstage, kids wander in and out, and parents stand on tall ladders, hanging a huge *Bayanihan* banner from the rafters.

I sit in a back row with Sheryl and Gracie and Alexa, who came by to hang out, too. Sheryl and I caught them up on everything. They feel just as disappointed that we can't build anymore.

"What else can we do?" Alexa asks.

I find a picture of Mr. Roger Rodrigo on my phone and show them. "This is the county tax collector."

"And?" Gracie says.

"And I'm going to convince him to cancel the auction." I smile. "People only get the things they want when they're bold and take action, right?"

"How?" Sheryl says.

"By showing him my house. I'm going to try to buy us more time for Mom to come up with the rest of the money or for me to finish building — or both."

The girls glance at each other.

"Ummm . . . I guess the worst he could say is . . . no?" Gracie says.

"Exactly."

"Have you already talked to him?" Sheryl asks.

"I've been calling, but I just get voice mail. I'm going to his office. I checked the map. I've been to that building with Lola when she had to pay parking tickets. It's not far. I won't be long."

"Maybe we should go with you," Gracie offers.

I brighten. "Sure! The more of us there are, the harder we'll be to ignore. He won't have any choice but to call the whole thing off."

"But Maribel's supposed to be here soon, and she'll see that we're gone," Sheryl says.

"Would she drive us?" I ask.

Sheryl thinks. "Maybe."

CHAPTER 19
SAY SOMETHING MORE

Maribel was in a good mood — and I'm persuasive.

The girls and I walk with Maribel out to the minivan. "So, Lou, inquiring minds want to know. Why go through all this trouble just for dirt and trees?" Maribel says.

"Because it belonged to half of me." Maribel was a little girl when Mom got pregnant, so she met Dad. "Do you remember what my dad was like?"

She nods. "He was nice, and funny, too.

He used to play Go Fish with me and Kelvin and he always let us win." Maribel smiles at me now. "Do what you need to do, little cuz."

"Thanks, Manang."

The plan: Maribel's telling Auntie that we stopped at the mall, Gracie's telling her mom she's at Sheryl's, Alexa's telling her mom she's at Gracie's. And Maribel's driving. We're covered.

I slide open the Filipino-Mobile and we help Sheryl up before piling in.

Professional-looking people walk up and down the glossy halls of the Civic Center. We look out of place in our sweats and dance clothes, but no one pays attention to us as we walk straight for the elevator and press the button to go up.

"I see some vending machines. I'll find you later," Maribel says. "Do you have an appointment with the guy?"

We jump into the elevator. "Do we need one?" Gracie asks. Maribel rolls her eyes.

Upstairs, our footsteps echo until Alexa stops us at a door.

Terra Vista County Department of Property Tax.

"Okay, big deep breath," I say, and we all inhale.

In the office, there's an older lady at the front desk and no one else waiting. She peers at us over her glasses. "May I help you?"

The girls stand behind me protectively, like backup dancers.

"Uh, hi. I was wondering if, um, if I could please talk to someone?" I say, more softly than I imagined myself doing.

"I'm sorry, I'm having a hard time hearing you," she says.

"I'd like to speak with Mr. Rodrigo, please."

"May I ask what this is regarding?"

"Well . . ."

Of all the times for a brain fart. The girls wait for me to convince her. It's my only chance, and I don't want to mess it up.

Sheryl steps in. "This is my cousin Lucinda Bulosan-Nelson. She has some questions about her property."

"Yes, very important questions," Gracie says.

"About tax collection," Alexa adds.

The lady seems confused, but finally I find my voice. Sometimes it hides, but it comes out when I need it. That's what counts.

"I'd like to discuss a property auction."

"Is there an adult here with you?" the woman asks.

"No, I'm here representing my own property. I'd like to speak with the person in charge."

Her face softens. "I'm sorry, girls, but Mr. Rodrigo is on a call. You'll have to make an appointment and come back another time."

"Okay, she'll make an appointment, then," Alexa says.

"Yeah, pronto," Gracie says. Sheryl elbows her. "I mean please."

The woman clicks on a mouse and looks at her computer. "It seems that the earliest I have is four months from now."

"Four months? My land will be gone by then! The auction —" I stop. The girls glance at each other.

"Isn't there anything sooner?" Sheryl asks politely, and the lady clicks some more but shakes her head.

"It's all right, I understand," I say. "Thank you for your time."

"Are you sure?" Sheryl whispers. The girls give me questioning looks, but I nudge them in the direction of the Exit sign.

"Don't worry about it. Let's just go," I say.

I let the girls start walking away and before anyone can stop me, I charge past the receptionist to the closed door behind her and knock.

She jumps up. "Young lady, what are you doing?"

"Go, Lou!" Gracie says.

The door opens and a man steps out. "Yes?"

"I'm sorry, Roger, these young ladies asked to see you, but I've informed them that they need to —"

"Mr. Rodrigo, my name is Lucinda Bulosan-Nelson. I was hoping for a moment of your time. It's very important."

"Excuse me?"

"Please. You can make a decision that will affect my whole life."

He looks surprised. I surprised myself. I give my most confident smile. His eyes go back and forth from the receptionist to me.

"Please, sir, I promise to be brief," I say nicely.

"Of course. Step into my office." He opens the door wide.

Mr. Rodrigo likes baseball. There's a gigantic black-and-orange San Francisco Giants flag on the wall, and pictures of fun stuff like him tandem skydiving with two thumbs up.

I think he'll give me a shot.

He sits at his desk and we stand in front. The girls form a horseshoe around me.

"So what's this all about, kids?"

"You can't sell my land," I say. "The property on Stone Canyon Drive out in Terra Vista Valley, sir."

"Are you sure Marge didn't put you up to this?" He points toward the receptionist's desk and chuckles. I give him a serious look to show that I'm not pranking.

"Please, Mr. Rodrigo, you have to cancel that auction."

"Lucinda, I apologize, but the only way my office would not move forward would be for the owner of your land to pay what is owed by the deadline."

"We'll have it for you — my mom's working on it, and I'm helping. If you give me a little more time, I'll raise the rest of the money. I just need a chance."

"Is there someone I can call to pick you girls up?" he asks.

He's not hearing me; he only sees someone who doesn't know what she's doing. I yank the phone from my backpack and rush up to his desk.

"Okay, Mr. Rodrigo, picture this. A tiny house," I say, playing the video Jack made. "That's me, and all the people I love, working on it."

He watches the video as the girls and I watch him, but it's hard to figure out what he's thinking. At the end of the video he asks, "Is this on your property?"

I nod. "It's what my dad left for me. I never knew him, but I have our land. He was going to build our house there, but he passed away, and now it's my turn."

"And she can do it, you know?" Alexa says.

"Totally. Lou has the brainpower —" Gracie says.

"— and the muscle power," Sheryl adds. "Sometimes people underestimate kids, but Lou can do this. More than anyone we know."

I swipe through pictures of my heart collage and blueprint, and of women I admire who create things. The last images show different angles of my house-to-be, surrounded by friends.

"The front door goes here, the ladder to the sleeping loft there, and this corner's the special reading nook. I bet you didn't know you could fit so much into the smallest space, huh?"

Without asking, he swipes through the

pictures himself.

Convince him, Lou. Say something more.

"Do you have any kids, Mr. Rodrigo?"

He gives me an odd look, but he nods. We all smile.

"That's great! May I ask you something?" I say.

"Sure, go ahead."

"Let's pretend you have a daughter and you've given her something that means the world to you. But suddenly you have to leave, and it's not your fault, but you'll never see her again. Shouldn't she have something to know you by?"

Mr. Rodrigo clasps his hands and looks directly at me.

"Lucinda, this is very unconventional. I can tell you're a smart young lady, but this matter is something I would need to discuss with your mother since she has guardianship of the property. She should contact my office." He hands me a business card. "I appreciate you all coming by, but I'm afraid I have another meeting."

I've lost my shot. He was supposed to

shake my hand and say, "Calling off the auction! The land's all yours!" Instead, he's opening the door.

"Thanks for your time. Let's go," I say to the girls.

We stand outside in the hallway. What now?

I wish I could get to my best thinking spot. I check the time. "I'm going to the land." Mom will be angry, but I have to.

"Right now?" Gracie asks.

"I know it sounds strange, but when I'm out there, it's like my dad's with me. Maybe he can tell me what to do, give me some sort of a sign."

"Should we all go?" Sheryl asks.

I shake my head. "I don't want to get everyone in trouble. But thanks for all your help in there. You were amazing." I smile at them.

The elevator at the end of the long hall opens and Maribel steps out.

"Tell Manang I'm in the bathroom. I'll be fine getting home."

The girls look at each other like they're

not sure how far to take this for me. Maribel heads our way.

"Quick, hide," Alexa says.

Gracie opens the door to a random office and shoves me in.

"May I help you?" a man says. I stand there, frozen.

I can hear them through the door as Maribel asks, "How'd it go? Where's Lou?"

"She's . . . in the bathroom. She'll meet us at the van," Sheryl says.

That was close.

As soon as I think they're gone, I wave to the surprised man at the desk and slip out.

A stairway exit!

I run down four flights as fast as I can, exiting somewhere on the opposite side of where we parked. Perfect.

Now, where's the bus stop? I spot it across the street.

Cars jet quickly in both directions and I wait for the road to clear. Minutes feel like hours until it's safe for me to cross. I sprint over and my bus pulls up right on time: Route 143.

Passengers step off.

I'm out of breath.

Almost there.

"Lou! What are you doing?" Maribel yells from across the street. The girls are stopped at a red light as more traffic whizzes by.

I hear their shouts:

"Hurry, Lou!"

"We tried to stall!"

I glance at the bus driver, but he doesn't seem to notice.

"You better not get on that bus!" Maribel yells, but I step on and the doors clamp shut. I take a seat all the way in back.

Maribel runs across, Sheryl limping behind with Alexa and Gracie.

"Sir, please, I'm in a hurry, can you go now?" I shout to the driver, but he's checking his phone. Maribel makes it to the door and pounds on it.

"Hey, young lady, take it easy," the driver says, holding his hand up.

The doors open.

"Sorry, I just need to grab my little cousin — she's not supposed to be here," Maribel says, charging toward me with her you're-in-huge-trouble-now face.

The passengers watch as she drags me off.

Chapter 20
The Way We Always Do

At home, I have nowhere to hide. I sink into the couch while Mom paces. She stops and gives me her best disappointed look. I hate that look.

"This is so unlike you, Lou."

"I was trying to save things!"

"By barging in on a county official?" Maribel told her everything.

"I had to. I can't lose my land."

"Lucinda, you may not cross the bridge again on your own, or take the bus, or do anything else without my permission."

"Can I at least show you my house?"

"This is the end of any house talk."

"But, Mom —"

"You're grounded — again. The only thing you're allowed to do until we move is dance practice."

"Don't you even want to know what I'm talking about? Can you please come see?"

Mom lets out a sigh and sits next to me. I watch her face soften.

"Oh, Lou, all this auction stuff . . . it's a lot to deal with, huh? I'm trying to fix everything so your land doesn't get sold — I want you to know that — but it's not okay for you to be running around wherever you like."

"I'm sorry, Mom," I say. And I am. But I need her to understand, to see what I've done — even if it won't change her mind about moving.

"May I ask you something?" She nods. "Have I ever done anything I wasn't supposed to? I've always done what I'm supposed to as part of this family, right?"

She puts her arm around me and I look

her in the eyes.

"Please, can I just show you what I'm talking about? It's important to me. Then I'm one hundred percent grounded," I say, crossing an X over my heart.

Mom pauses for what feels like forever.

"Go get your jacket," she says.

I can't remember the last time I saw Mom out here. She notices the trailer bed and I peel the tarp off so she can finally see.

"So this is the reason you've been sneaking out here, huh?" she says, surprised.

"Yeah. Annie and Mr. Keller helped me a ton, and so did Sheryl and Arwin and our friends. It's the base. Phase one." I smile.

"Gosh, Lou, you really built this?" she says, touching the planks like they're precious. "You have the same gift that your dad did, you know? I'm proud of you, honey. He would be, too." She hugs me.

I sit on my subfloor with Mom.

"My meeting at the county office is

scheduled now. I'll be talking to them the day before Barrio Fiesta. I wish it was sooner," she says.

"Then what happens?"

"Then we work something out, the way we always do."

"Are you sure?"

"Absolutely. We never stop. I learned that from your grandparents and all the other *lolos* and *lolas*."

Mom rises and peers around, resting her fists on her waist the way a superhero might. She notices the shed with its doors slightly open from the wind. "May I look in there?"

I nod.

While she's inside, I try to imagine how good it will feel to pound in the last nail.

"Got something for us," Mom says, carrying out the box I found when I first pried the shed open. "I think these may be old family movies that belonged to the Nelsons. Let's take them home. Keep them safe."

"If you want."

"There's another place we should go today."

■ ■ ■ ■

As soon as we reach the bottom of the hill, I know.

"Dad," I say.

Mom nods. She's driven us to the cemetery where the Nelson family is buried. We park, and an easy walking trail leads us to a beautiful, wide view of Mount Tam. I open the gate.

"A visit might help us," she says.

We weave through lines of headstones and grass. The only sounds are birds, a plane overhead, and leaves rattling across the grass like crumpling paper.

Mom stops at three markers made from a speckly granite — *Theodore Nelson, Beverly Nelson, Michael Nelson.* Together we kneel and she carefully touches each stone.

There's something calming about knowing that they're here, near me.

"Did I ever tell you that Lola didn't want me to go to Michael's funeral?" she says.

"How come?"

"Oh, one of her annoying superstitions. You were still in my belly. It had something to do with a baby getting bad luck if the mother looks at the dead."

"How'd you convince her to let you go?"

"I told her there wouldn't be an open casket. Your dad was cremated, not like the kind of family services you've been to."

"What was his funeral like?"

"A few relatives and close friends. Beautiful prayers. People gave little speeches about him, and Grandpa Ted and I held hands. Gemma called it very tasteful." She pauses. "Ted and I were still . . . in shock . . . the accident." Her voice gets soft and trails off.

I think of Lolo's funeral, which stays sharp in my mind. He wore a *barong,* a sheer ivory shirt made from pineapple fabric that Filipinos wear to weddings and baptisms and things. Thin black veils covered the *lolas'* faces as they clutched their rosaries and wept loudly over his casket. Some people even took pictures of Lolo or leaned in to kiss his cheek. Mom and Auntie did, and it freaked out the cousins and me.

Afterward, Lola announced that for her death she wanted a FUNeral and for all the guests to sing Michael Jackson songs and eat a mango sheet cake with her face on it. Everyone laughed. She cheered up the room even though we should have been doing that for her.

Mom plucks at grass and stares off somewhere. "Want to hear something?"

She shares a piece of my history I never knew — that Lolo and Lola didn't want her and Dad to get married. They thought she was too young and she should finish college first. They said Mom didn't need some white guy she just met to help raise me.

But somehow Lola and Lolo changed their minds, realized that's not what families do. Families support. They carry houses on their shoulders during floods, no matter how heavy or hard. So even though Dad's family seemed different, the three grandparents agreed they had to help out in every way.

"That's how the Bulosans and the Nelsons got to know each other." Mom smiles. "And that's why you and I moved in with Grandpa Ted and why we live with Lola now. I complain sometimes, but her home is ours. Wherever we end up, it always will be."

"Do you think Dad really would have built us a house?" I ask.

"No question."

I love it when she talks about him.

Mom hooks my hair behind my ear. I ask her what I can't get out of my head: "What if the tax people say no?"

"I've been working out a settlement plan to propose, and Auntie Gemma helped me with the numbers. That's basically a down payment to buy us some time while I come up with the rest. It's going to work."

"Where are you getting the money?"

"I've been saving — even Lola's helping. I sold the car. The person who's buying it still has to come pick it up."

"What? Oh my gosh, Mom, why?"

"It's okay, we never use it. Listen, don't worry about any of this — that's my job."

I remember the empty box in her filing cabinet. "Did you sell your ring?"

"How did you know about that?" Before I can explain, she pulls a necklace out from under her shirt, a golden circle dangling at its end. "I almost did, but . . . I couldn't."

Lolo used to tell us stories of the *manongs,* thousands of men who came from the Philippines to California way before Mom and I were ever born. They left everything they knew to take hard jobs in factories and farms for ten cents an hour, ten hours a day, even though signs around town greeted them with three words: *No Filipinos Allowed.* "They sent money home. Every hardship they endured was for their families," Lolo would say.

Sometimes I complain about my family, too, but I know they'd do anything for each other. My mom's amazing. She's doing this all for me.

We rise and stretch and a few others walk through the cemetery, some bringing flowers. Mom gently places her warm hands on my cheeks. "One day you'll finish your tiny house."

One day.

I wish it could be now, but Mom's

already brought home empty packing boxes and has started looking for a place to rent in Washington. She says by the time I start eighth grade I'll have my own room, but that's the last thing I want now.

"I almost forgot!" She reaches into her purse and pulls out a small white envelope with *Lucinda* written on it in happy, shouty colors.

"It's your birthday gift from Lola and me, a little early."

I open it. Inside sits a thick piece of cardstock, a gift certificate that says *One-Day Workshop in the Art of the Tiny House.*

I've heard about this class at the community college. I've always wanted to do it, but I never asked because I thought she'd say no or that we didn't have the money.

"I'm working that day, but Annie said she'd love to take you. I hope that's okay."

"Thanks, Mom." I hold her tightly.

Chapter 21
Move Away

My dance group sits onstage, decked out in full Barrio Fiesta gear like a rainbow. We've had a long morning of practice, and everyone's ready to go home.

How strange to think that by the end of summer, "home" won't mean Lola's. Not being able to visit my land or work on my house means that now I can think only of leaving. Annie said we could store my trailer bed on her lot. Even if I get to keep my land, I still have to say goodbye.

"Dancers, this is it, last dress rehearsal!

Next weekend, this will be for real! Tell me what that means," Miss Jovy says. Arwin shoots his hand up and she points to him.

"Don't fart onstage once it gets quiet for our number?"

The kids hoot and holler.

"Yes, definitely what Arwin said. But it also means that I need every one of you to give this your best effort. If you mess up, just keep going," she says, looking straight at me. "Let's go, places, please! And put on those performance faces!"

The pole holders line their thick bamboo reeds flat on the floor, and we plaster on big smiles. Cue the music.

I hop in and manage a few steps — *hooray!* — until my ankle catches on a reed. Everyone keeps dancing around me.

I wait for a beat to leap back in but I can't seem to find it. The others jump and twirl into and out of the poles while I stand off to the side. Soon the song's finished. I haven't even left California yet, and already they've moved on without me.

■ ■ ■ ■

Mom and I get home from practice. Lola's fluttering about the garage — shifting, opening, plucking things from boxes. She holds up a can of Spam and reads the date. "Expired two years ago. It's probably still good!" She laughs her crazy laugh and tosses it into a box. "I'm getting some *balikbayan* boxes ready to send home."

"Who's going this time?" Mom asks, and as she walks into the house, Lola shouts: "Your uncle AJ's wife's third cousin's hairdresser. You remember him?"

Whenever my family talks about "going home," they mean the Philippines.

"Can I help, Lola?" I ask.

"You know what to do!" She slides over a huge box and hands me a tape gun.

My whole life I've watched Lola pack these. A *balikbayan* means someone who doesn't live in the Philippines. A *balikbayan* box is what gets sent to family who still live there. The boxes travel with someone flying home.

Lola includes all kinds of things: big coffee tins, mass quantities of toothpaste, shoes, clothes, and lipstick in pretty shades for all the aunties there.

I shut the flaps and stretch a long piece of tape over the seam before patting it down.

Mom peeks into the garage and says, "Lou, I got a voice mail from Mr. K. He had something important to tell us. Do you know what that's about?"

"Nope."

She sits on the doorstep and dials.

"Hi, Peter, it's Minda. Got your message." She listens. "No problem, you're on speaker." She holds the phone up and says, "Lou and Celina are here, too."

"Helloooo, ladies! Can you hear me?" he asks.

"Loud and clear, Peety!" Lola shouts.

"I have some fantastic news, so brace yourselves!"

"We're listening!" I say.

"Okay, because you, Ms. Lucinda Bulosan-Nelson, were nominated for Channel Forty's Student of the Year

Award by me, your favorite teacher of all time, Mr. Peter Keller."

What's he talking about?

"And you won!" he says.

"What? What did we win?" Lola asks.

"The chance to be on TV! Bay Area Channel Forty. Do you ladies watch them in the morning? They have a yearly contest. No student I've ever nominated has been chosen . . . until now. We won! Isn't that tremendous? I get to be on the telly with you!"

"Ay susmaryosep!" Lola says. Jesus, Mary, and Joseph. She says that when she's surprised. Mom and I turn to each other and laugh, as giddy as Mr. K.

"Do you think I should go for a three-piece suit on camera, or perhaps my denim overalls to show off my rugged style?" he asks.

"Peter, gosh! You're one of a kind. Thank you so much! This is thrilling!" Mom says, hugging me. "But . . . *denim*?"

"Minda, they'd like to interview us next Friday. I'll give you all the details. Of course, only if it's something you'd like to participate in, Lou, and if your mother thinks it's appropriate?"

I nod to Mom.

Lola hooks her arm with mine and we spin, tape guns in the air, around our homebound boxes.

I sit in my closet and phone the girls to share the news. Alexa says, "I can't wait to choose your outfit!"

I laugh. "Okay," I say, and we end our call. One more to make.

Hearing from Mr. Keller reminded me of something Jack said. I stare at my phone, trying not to stop myself since what I'm about to do might cause lifelong embarrassment. I clamp my eyes shut, hold my breath . . . and dial.

The phone barely rings when he says, "Hey."

"Hi, Jack. I mean, hey. It's me . . . um, Lou." A long pause until finally I blurt out, "Did you have something to do with Mr. K and a news station contest?"

"Did you win?"

"Yes! Actually, it's more like Mr. Keller won. He was super excited," I say, and we both laugh.

"Nubby asked me if he could use some of the footage I filmed."

Bingo. Now I know. "So your video was the secret weapon, huh?" I feel myself getting a little embarrassed. "Thanks for doing that."

There's a pause, and I'm glad I can't see his face. Then he says, "Hey, guess what? I figured out the movie for my film-camp application. It's a mini-documentary. I call it: 'Frank's Diner . . . Burgers, Donuts, Kimchi Breakfast Burritos, and More!' Catchy, huh?"

"That sounds awesome."

"But I'm already screwed."

"Why?"

"Frank's letting me interview him tomorrow, but Carver Jamison just bailed. He was my assistant director!"

"Typical."

"My dad said I should film on my own because that's what 'auteur directors' do, but I don't really want to. I'll need more help."

"So what are you going to do?"

"I was kind of thinking about when we were out on your land and every-thing. . . ." Jack pauses. "And I was wondering if you'd want to be on my crew?"

"Me?"

"It's okay, forget it."

"No, hold on, I'll help. That's what friends are for, right?" He doesn't answer. *Shoot.* Did I just make things weird? "Then we can call it even," I add.

"You're on."

Alexa's mom drops us off in Sausalito at Frank's Diner, a little mom-and-pop hole-in-the-wall with red vinyl barstools and a sweet view of the bay. I recruited Alexa because awkward conversations feel better with a buddy. There's some-thing about Jack where sometimes I feel like me around him, but other times I get panicky, like I'm saying all the wrong things.

We walk in and Jack's setting up lights and fancy camera equipment. "Hey, you showed up."

"Of course . . . because we're here!" I say.

Facepalm.

Alexa gives me a grin. The long counter is stacked with plates of juicy hamburgers, old-fashioned milk shakes, and seven-layer cakes under glass domes.

"Whoa, those look yummy," I say.

Jack jumps in front of the food. "Step away from the props."

"So am I gonna be in this movie or not?" Alexa asks, pulling out a mirror and smearing on lip gloss with her pinky.

"Nope. You're the gaffer," he says, handing her a light on a tall pole. He opens and shuts a black-and-white clapper board and hands it to me. "Know how to use one of these? Not as fancy as a circular saw."

"I can probably figure it out."

My first time making a movie is fun. Jack interviews Frank and films customers eating while I follow him around with a microphone. Sometimes I bump into him and shout out "Sorry!" so that he has to yell "Cut!" It makes us laugh.

"We need more action shots," Jack says. "Any ideas?"

"Ummm . . . milk-shake race?" I say, pointing to the food on the counter.

"Good one!" Jack says. "You and Alexa can stand behind the bar."

"I was more thinking of you doing the race . . . and me filming," I say.

"Okay, but don't mess up," he says, handing over the camera. Jack shows me how to zoom in and out before we recruit a couple of customers to join him and Alexa.

I count them down, "Three, two, one . . . go!" and they all sip as fast as they can until Jack drains his glass first.

"We have a winner!" I shout, running over to him and pulling up his arm.

"You're supposed to be filming," he says, laughing. "But I can still use that."

By the end of the afternoon, I'm not so nervous around him anymore. Until he waves me over. "Want to see?" he asks.

Jack's sitting on one of the tall stools and I hop up beside him. He presses Play on his computer and we crack up at all the outtakes, like me crossing my eyes while clapping the clapper board.

"You're pretty good at this," I say, sitting close to him so I can see the screen. Our shoulders touch. He doesn't move away.

CHAPTER 22
NEVER HAD A CHANCE

It's early morning as Lola and I drive with Mr. Keller to the TV station for our special day. They chitchat for the whole ride. My knee bounces up and down, I can't get it to stop. I wish Mom could have come, but she's working. Right after her shift, she heads to her meeting at the county tax office.

Last night I had the worst nightmare: I was on live TV with Mr. Keller but suddenly the station turned into a stage. Bamboo poles morphed into snakes, slithering up my ankles, with thousands of people in the audience pointing at me. Then Mr. Keller shape-shifted into Mr. Rodrigo, who pounded an auction gavel, and the dream ended with Mom and me skydiving into Washington State.

Yikes!

"You ready, Lucinda?" Mr. Keller asks as we pull into the parking lot.

I pull at a thread on my skirt. Alexa's skirt, actually. The girls came over early and helped me get ready. I didn't want to dress so frilly, but I didn't have time to change before Mr. Keller picked us up.

We get out of the car. Mr. Keller's wearing a sharp suit, plus a tie with hammers on it.

"How do I look?" he asks.

"Snazzy!" I straighten his lapel and try not to pay attention to my prickly nerves as we head inside.

This is the coolest.

I'm sitting on a set that looks like someone's living room. The studio has tall cameras with people standing behind them and lots of other people with clip-boards and earpieces running around like there's an emergency. I'm surprised at how small the studio is — it looks bigger on TV. Jack will want to hear all about this.

Lola and the other kids' parents stand across the way where the camera can't see them; she gives me a little wave and a smile.

A blond lady sits in a leather chair on a platform with potted green plants and a coffee table complete with a coffee mug. She sips and looks at notes on white index cards.

When we got here, she said, "I'm Mo-rina, the *Good Day, Bay!* host," and she vigorously shook all the teachers' hands and gave us kids perky high fives.

Morina is wearing a lime-green suit topped with a baubly necklace. She has the most perfect helmet hair and the straightest, whitest teeth I've ever seen. She almost doesn't look real.

"We'll be starting soon, kids," she whispers excitedly. She picks her teeth with her pinky. "Any arugula stuck in there, or am I in the clear?"

I give her a thumbs-up. "You're good."

There are three winners. We sit across from the anchor, our teachers standing behind us. A woman holding a clipboard and wearing a headset shouts, "In three . . . two . . . one . . . We're rolling, people!"

The entire set is quiet. Morina repeats her blinding smile for the camera.

"And we're back with my favorite news story of the year! We ask teachers all over Northern California to nominate the student they believe exemplifies a leader of tomorrow, and I am thrilled to be sitting here with three of our local best and brightest . . . our winners!"

Morina shouts *"Woooooooooo!"* as the behind-the-scenes people clap.

I can't believe I'm up here. My smile is huge.

"I am so happy to welcome you to the show."

"And we're so happy to be here, Morina!" Mr. Keller says, beating everyone else to speaking first. This is his moment and I'm happy for him.

Morina introduces us.

The first winner is an eighth-grade boy with a pink Mohawk who gives haircuts to homeless people. The other winner is a girl in fourth grade who teaches advanced calculus to college kids. Holy guacamole.

Morina chats with the boy, then the girl. The screen behind her shows clips of each kid in action. I'm in a daze where I can't hear what she's saying or how the other winners respond, even though I can see their mouths moving.

Morina turns to me.

"Lucinda Bulosan-Nelson. Am I pronouncing that correctly?"

I manage to say "Yup."

"May I call you Lou?" I nod. "You were nominated by your seventh-grade Industrial Arts and Technology teacher from Rizal Middle School, Peter Keller."

Mr. Keller waves to the camera with his good hand. "I've nominated a student every year for thirty years, and you've finally made the right choice. You're lucky I stuck with you people for so long." Morina laughs.

"Lou, your goal here is most intriguing. . . . I understand you're building . . . a tiny house?"

"Yup." It's all I can muster with a room of big cameras and bright lights staring at me. It's not like when Jack films.

"This is such a coincidence, because I am completely addicted to the home and design channels and I've heard about these itty-bitty homes. Although where do you go to the bathroom?" she says, cackling. "Let's take a quick look at what Lou's been up to."

Behind her on set is a humongous screen where I see myself: sawing, hammering, and blowing bangs out of my eyes as I concentrate. Jack's footage.

Close-ups capture different hands gripped around tools, and sawdust flying like confetti. Shots show my friends acting silly and having fun.

The camera zooms in on my face and I cringe, spotting pimples and stray hairs. But it's me, it's who I am, filling up the screen.

Finally, the camera zooms in on my hands, pounding at a nail, before it turns upward into the skyline with trees like umbrellas and the whole thing fades.

"I am loving your creativity," Morina says. "Tell me more, Lou. Why are you building this? Why a tiny house?"

I have to think about it. The camera's red light points at me and I freeze — I'm not sure what to say. Morina waits, but I'm stuck.

"Lucinda has a unique knack for bringing her ideas to life," Mr. Keller says.

"Because I want to have my own house on my own land!" I shout, to my surprise, in front of *everyone.* I can feel my cheeks turning hot.

Mr. Keller puts his hands on my shoulders and I feel him give an encouraging squeeze. I look up at him and he smiles at me.

Morina laughs and says into the camera, "A house is made of wood, folks, but a home is made of dreams. You heard it here."

A home is made of dreams? Not at all. I know a lot better than that now.

A guy wearing a headset carries out three giant cardboard rectangles and hands one to each winner. They all say

Good Day, Bay! Student of the Year. And the best part? The amount says *Five Hundred Dollars.* What?

The teachers shake each other's hands and Haircut Kid, Calculus Girl, and I look at each other with shocked faces.

"Congratulations! For Channel Forty, I'm Morina Medrano!" A voice somewhere yells, "Cut!"

After the taping, Mr. Keller, Lola, and I go home to a house full of family, cheers, and hugs. I glance around for Mom. I'm ready for her good news so we can really celebrate.

"Is she back yet?" I ask.

Auntie Gemma shakes her head. "You were terrific, Lou."

"Those big cameras were terrifying. I hardly said anything!"

"I can't wait to help you spend that five hundred bucks," Arwin says, and we laugh as everyone gathers around the table to fill up their plates.

"I'll use it for my land to pay off the taxes. I can still stop the auction!" I whisper to Sheryl.

"What auction?" Uncle Felix, one of my mom's cousins, asks. I don't look his way.

"The city's going to sell Lou's land," Arwin says. Sheryl elbows him. Hard.

"Hi, sorry I'm a little late!" Mom's at the door. She holds her arms out to me. "Oh, come here, you. I can't wait to see the recording."

"You're going to be very proud of her, Minda," Mr. Keller says.

"But what's all this about an auction for Lou's land?" Uncle Felix asks.

Mom looks surprised. "How do you know about that?"

"I overheard the kids," he says.

"Are you having financial difficulties, Minda? Is there a way we can help?" asks Auntie Jing, his wife.

Mom tries to laugh and shrug it off, but I can tell she's embarrassed.

"I didn't mean anything by it. I was just nervous," I say.

"Sheryl said that Auntie Minda owes a bunch of money, and that's why they're holding the auction," Arwin says.

"Hoy!" Auntie Gemma says in her best Filipino scowl. "That's none of your concern."

"Come on, everybody! Time for more food! We all need some good energy for the festival tomorrow." Lola pushes people toward the food table to give us some privacy.

Mom says quietly to Auntie Gemma, "I didn't want everyone to know yet."

"Min, they're only asking because they're concerned. We all want to help," Auntie says.

"How was your meeting? What did they say?" I ask.

Mom whispers, "Honey, we can talk about it after everyone goes home."

"Is the auction canceled?" She doesn't seem happy like I thought she would.

"You okay, sis?" Auntie asks softly.

"They called it off, right? You saw Mr. Rodrigo?"

Mom shakes her head. "No, Lou, I didn't. I met with other people from his office." She tries to smile. "Hey, let's celebrate. I want to hear all about the news station."

"But I've been waiting all day."

Mom looks from Auntie to me. There's a long silence until she finally says, "Lou . . . I couldn't make it work. I thought they'd accept the amount I was able to offer but . . . they didn't."

"What are you saying?"

"The auction's still going to happen."

No. I feel sick.

"I'm so sorry. But listen, I got lots of great information and I have a few more ideas," she says.

"Why don't you go talk on the patio? No one's out there," Auntie says.

"They're still going to hold the auction?" I ask. Both of them look at me sadly. "They're selling my land?"

I run into the bedroom, but Arwin and some of the little cousins are jumping on the beds. I try my closet, but Maribel's in there texting.

"Hey," she says. I shut the door on her.

This isn't happening. It can't be.

Maribel leaves the closet and I take her place, shutting the door behind me. I close my eyes, but I can't block out the noise.

After a while, Lola comes in and says, "Okay, *anaks,* time for everybody to get some rest now. Let's go, let's go . . . big day tomorrow! Barrio Fiesta!"

Operation Tiny House Fail.

In my closet, piece by piece, I pry away parts of my heart, stripping off every picture, shredding them down, building little paper piles as the tape sticks to my nails. All these wishes that never had a chance.

Someone knocks on my door. I don't feel like talking to Mom right now.

"Hey, it's us," voices say.

The door creaks a sliver and three sets of eyes appear: Sheryl, Alexa, and Gracie.

"Can we come in?" Sheryl asks.

They pull the door open and Gracie's eyes widen. "Oh my gosh, Lou, why did you do that to your vision heart?" She picks up the torn pieces and tries to pat them back up, but they fall.

"All righty, all righty . . . move over,

move over . . . ," Alexa says.

They squish in and sit.

"We came to cheer you up," Sheryl says.

"These should help." Alexa holds up a clear bag of cookies. She hands one to each of us and we bite in. "Avocado cacao chip. My mom's secret recipe."

They giggle, but it's hard for me to laugh. When they see that I don't, they all get quiet.

"Well, so what if we kept building?" Gracie asks.

"Yeah, you could build it on Annie's lot. She'd let you," Sheryl says.

I know they're trying to help, but there's nothing more I can do. We're moving. I lost my land.

"I don't have anything left," I say.

"You still have us," Sheryl says.

"And . . . you still have Jack Allen," Alexa jokes.

I begin to cry. Nobody says a word. Alexa bites into another cookie.

They stare at the floor and let me cry. I know I have the best friends when even their silence makes me feel better.

I wipe my eyes. "How am I going to dance tomorrow?"

"Oh, I know, we can drop some wood on your foot and then maybe you won't have to!" Gracie says.

Sheryl starts to laugh — and so do Alexa and Gracie. They link their arms around me and together we knock heads.

"Will you promise to come visit after we move?" I say.

"Yes!" they shout.

CHAPTER 23
HOW IT WORKS

The senior center's parking lot bustles with action. Volunteers set up tables and large white tents. Uncles in aprons start up the grills, and delicious smells waft through. Booths line the lot, selling old things, new things, crafts and jewelry and vintage *barongs* — you name it.

I'm at a table with Gracie and some other girls from our dance group. We all wear Hawaiian shirts and leis over our costumes, and the banner I painted says *Sari-Sari Store* in bright blue, yellow, and red letters, the colors of the Philippine flag.

Sari-sari means "variety." Lola loves to tell us her memories of these colorful little stores and shacks in the Philippines where everyone stops for sodas and treats on hot, humid days. We're selling squares of her sweet, sticky rice cakes, plus drinks. Gracie pushes soda cans into a cooler of ice, then gives a little hula shake. "We look pretty fab if I do say so myself."

I try to seem excited — but who am I kidding? Mom's arranging for the uncles to move everything — the shed and my flatbed — to Annie's lot for storage. Annie said that one day I'll find another building spot, but I don't know about that.

"You okay?" Gracie asks.

"We gave it a good shot, huh?" I say, and she hugs me.

Lola's manning tables full of rummage-sale items. She waves both arms at me from across the lot and I go over to see her.

A woman walks up to us holding out a

purse. Our first customer.

"How much?" she asks.

The bag's brand-new; it still has the tags. I grab the little paper rectangle and read it. "According to the original price . . . eighty bucks. But we're charging half."

"I'll give you ten," she says. I'm about to say yes when Lola steps in.

"Sixty," Lola says forcefully.

"Fifteen," the lady says, just as aggressively.

"Fifty-five."

"Twenty."

"Forty. This is designer. Never used. Looks good in the nightclubs," Lola says. "I can tell you understand the value of this, so please do not insult me." Her final offer.

"She's good," the lady says to me, forking over the cash.

As the woman walks away, Lola whispers, "I would have taken five." We laugh. Then she says, "I've been searching for your mama. Have you seen her?"

"I think she's backstage helping Miss Jovy."

"Come on, let's go find her and your auntie Gemma." Lola grabs my hand. "There's something we need to share with you both."

Miss Jovy runs through the parking lot frantically, gathering stray kids. She points at me. "You! Dressing room! Now!"

"It's okay, we'll do it later," Lola says, giving me a smile and a nudge toward the auditorium.

A dark stage, barely lit, covered by a large screen.

My group and I wait in the wings, lined up in our bright costumes, everyone barefoot. The girls wear their hair in tight low buns and the boys have kerchiefs around their necks.

I've been dancing in this festival since I was little, but this part always feels the same: stomach somersaults and trembly legs. I take deep breaths and try to push the other stuff from my mind.

Arwin turns around and loud-whispers, "Are you nervous?" I shush him.

A slow beat begins. That's our cue.

The pole holders walk onstage first, carrying the long bamboo reeds, their silhouettes on the screen the only thing visible to the audience. No music plays yet, just a steady beat, which the audience claps to. The pole holders reach their spots and assemble the poles in parallel lines on the floor.

The music begins with its joyful melody, starting soft, getting louder and louder.

We dancers sway out, single file. Slowly the screen rises and the lights brighten until our shadows fade. We hit our marks sharply.

The lights shine. The music stops.

It's quiet — until the clacking of wood to wood: *boom boom click boom boom click.* There's energy in the air.

I raise my flouncy skirt in time with the others and hop into and out of the reeds as the audience cheers.

Not a single person tripped or missed the beat, not even me! I'm so relieved. Happy sounds bounce off the walls as everyone gathers onstage — dancers, family, friends. It's a colossal Filipino party. People give flowers wrapped in plastic or take pictures next to the *bahay kubo.*

Alexa and her mom meet me, Mom, and Lola in the middle of the crowd.

"You guys were great!" Alexa says, and she and her mom give us hugs before Alexa runs off to congratulate her other friends.

Mom hands me a bouquet of red mums, which I cradle like a Miss Preteen Sampaguita. Mom's ring dangles from a golden chain around her neck, and the stage lights make the diamond twinkle.

"Oh, Lou, you were so much fun to watch. I remember dancing *Tinikling,* but I wasn't nearly as good as you kids."

"And you didn't fall up there, *anak.* Nice job," Lola says, patting my back.

Auntie Gemma and Sheryl rush toward us.

"There you are," Lola says to them.

Sheryl says, "We've been looking for you guys everywhere!"

Auntie holds an envelope out to Mom.

"For you and Lou."

My mom and I look at each other.

"What are you waiting for, Auntie? Open it!" Sheryl says.

Mom opens the envelope and pulls out a check.

"Oh my gosh, oh my gosh . . . ," Mom says, shocked.

"What is it?" I ask.

Auntie Gemma says, "If you add the amount to what you've already saved, you should have enough for the county. We held an emergency family meeting and everyone gave what they could."

Mom holds the check out to me — I'm just as stunned.

"This is so much money," Mom says.

"Even the community center donated a little, for all the help our family's given over the years," Auntie Gemma says.

Anak ko," Lola says, "we know how hard you've worked to take care of Lou, and we're so proud of you both. What happens to you and Lou matters to all of us. This is what we do for each other." Mom turns to Lola and holds her close.

I grab Mom's arm. "Can we still stop the auction?"

"I think so. I'll call the tax office now," Mom says. "And leave a message. They open on Monday. I can't believe this."

But actually, I can. I'd do anything for my family, too. We all know this is how it works.

I throw my arms around Sheryl and Auntie Gemma.

Mom and I are crying now — and laughing and hugging.

CHAPTER 24
SEE IT CLEARLY NOW

"What a day," Lola says with a smile. She sits on the couch, closing her eyes for a rest, and I join her. We've made it through another festival.

I'm not really sure what to feel right now — happy that the land's still mine, but sad that we have to move.

I'm tired. Time to veg out.

"My show's recorded. Is it okay if I watch?" I ask, and Lola nods.

I turn on the TV and find the title: *Get Decked Out.*

Mom walks in. "Fashion makeovers? I don't think I've seen this one before."

"No, it's construction TV, about building house decks."

"Oh, Lou," Mom says with an exaggerated groan, and we laugh. After everything, it feels great to do that.

"Popcorn?" I ask.

"Yes, please," Lola says.

I pause at the opening credits and run into the kitchen to grab the bowl.

"Loaded with butter," I say, setting it on the coffee table and stuffing a huge, salty handful in my mouth. I join Lola on the couch and spread a blanket across our laps.

Mom's hooking cables into the TV from a rectangular silver box.

"What's that?" I ask.

"A videocassette recorder, VCR for short. It's how your auntie and I used to watch movies. . . . But let's see if I can get this dinosaur to work." Mom presses buttons and says, "I lost some important tapes your dad and Grandpa Ted made a long time ago. I'm hoping the ones from the shed might be them."

She grabs a video from Dad's box and pushes it into the machine. The VCR clunks and swallows it up.

Mom joins us under the blanket, me in between, and points a remote. An image plays.

It's a little fuzzy. That's when I see him. *Him.*

It's my dad. He's on the screen, and he's moving. I've never been able to picture how he moved. Mom grabs my hand and squeezes.

Dad's right in front of the lens, fiddling and setting the camera onto a tripod.

Up close, Michael Nelson has pale skin and hair the color of mine, sandy brown, definitely not Filipino. He looks like a guy lost people might ask for directions from because he seems friendly.

Dad's wearing what I normally do, jeans and a T-shirt. He smiles into the camera. Weird; it's like he's looking at me. The frame shakes as he adjusts the lens, and after it steadies he walks backward, still peering my way.

Now I know why she fell in love with

him: My dad was handsome.

I'd recognize the setting anywhere — our land.

The orange hammock's strung between the same two trees, but it's brighter, not faded like it is now.

Please say something so I can hear your voice.

"Hello. I'm about to do the biggest, most important thing I've ever done in my life," he says.

His voice! He sounds kind. My heart is full, hearing it.

Dad reaches into his pocket and pulls out a small red box. He opens it up and shows off the ring, the one I know.

He waves goodbye and walks toward the camera again to turn it off. Our screen goes blank.

"Wait, come back!" Lola says, glued to the TV and eating popcorn like she's watching one of her soaps.

An image appears, and there's Michael Nelson again. He puts a finger up to his nose and looks into the camera as if he's saying "Shhhh."

Dad walks offscreen, the gravel and leaves crunching under his footsteps, then brings Mom in, blindfolded. He pushes her forward gently.

Mom clutches my hand even tighter.

He probably towers a good foot over her. They look so young. She's glowing, and her belly's rounded out.

"Where are you taking me?" she asks, laughing, as he walks her toward the hammock and helps her sit. They're not close to the camera, so it's a little hard to hear, but I'd recognize her laugh anywhere.

Dad slips the blindfold off and Mom seems surprised. He bends on one knee and lifts something for her to view up close — my dollhouse.

"It's gorgeous, Michael. Did you build this?" She peeks in.

He nods. "It's for Lucinda when she's a little older. Just the starter until I build our real house."

"Lucinda's going to love it. Our Lou."

"Lou?" he asks.

"That's what we'll call her. Do you like it?"

"It's perfect," he says, laughing. "Go ahead, look inside. Search the rooms."

She does, carefully, pulling out tiny models of furniture, admiring them, putting them back again. Until she finds another surprise: the red box.

Mom flips the top and covers her mouth. Dad places the dollhouse on the ground and slides the ring onto her finger as she nods and shrieks. He lifts her. The hammock swings wildly.

"She said yes!"

They both walk up to the camera, and all I see is her belly, round and full.

He kneels down a second time, but now it's to kiss her stomach.

I'm looking right into his eyes as he says, "Lou, I wanted you to have a memory of this moment. Your mom and I are making it official, and I can't wait to finally meet you, my sweet little girl." He puts his hand on her tummy and rubs for good luck.

In the video they're laughing and so happy. And it's strange, because now I see: I get my eyes from her, my nose from him, and my skin color from them both.

It's like I'm watching a dream. The tape ends.

Lola and Mom hold hands across my lap. They're crying — so am I.

"We would have made things work, Lou," Mom says.

For the rest of the night we watch more videos:

A room full of people wearing pointy party hats, blowing horns that swirl out and in; they surround my parents — their engagement party.

Mom in a hospital bed with a baby in her arms, Grandpa Ted's voice saying: "Mikey, my boy, I wish you were here with us. Your daughter is stunning."

Me with both grandpas in Lola's back-yard, building benches. The grandpas try to hammer, but I keep interrupting, dancing around to get their attention.

We watch all kinds of clips full of family in different places, but always the feeling's the same: of love, of home. No matter what house we're in, they always fill me with happiness.

"Amazing," Mom keeps saying softly.

We sit, hushed. Three generations holding hands.

Chapter 25
Something New

Moonlight travels in through the window and shines on Mom, in bed on her side of the room. She's not asleep, either.

Late at night, Lolo used to tell me and my cousins ghost stories in the dark. He'd turn the lights down low, which made it super spooky, and none of the cousins dared to interrupt as he'd talk about the souls of Philippine soldiers who died in World War II fighting for America, trudging through his village still searching for home. He said you could see the sadness in their faces from having lived through so much destruction. Whenever I'm in the dark, I remember those tales. They still freak me out a little.

"Are you awake, sweetie?" Mom asks.

"I'm up."

"What are you thinking about?"

I'm thinking about my dad, how his eyes moved when he smiled, and about his voice, which was easy to listen to.

I'm thinking about my land, and how it feels just right to build there.

I'm thinking about tomorrow, when I turn thirteen, and a couple of weeks after that, when we leave — and how everyone has said that one day I'll build again.

But I tell her what I'm thinking most: "I don't want to say goodbye to everything."

Mom has her hands behind her head, staring at the ceiling, and I can hear her sighing, sighing.

In the morning the doorbell rings, and when I answer, it's Sheryl, Gracie, and Alexa wearing party dresses and huge smiles.

"Happy birthday!" they shout in unison, throwing their arms up like a synchronized act.

"Thank you, thank you, thank you," I say, and they're so goofy and giggly that I join in.

"Let's get you ready!" Alexa hands me a dress, something straight out of a teen magazine, and pushes me in the direction of my closet. "First, put that on. Second, we're going somewhere. Someplace top-secret."

"I don't do dresses, you know that."

"See, I told you she wouldn't," Gracie says.

Alexa sighs. "You were right."

"But that's why we came prepared." Sheryl hands me something else — a tool belt — but in the pockets, pretty flowers and ribbons poke out in soft colors.

"Oh my gosh, I've always wanted one." It's not even girl-ified in pink or with swirly designs like I've seen; it's just a plain old regular belt to hold my tools when I build. It's a little worn, and somehow familiar.

"I took it from Lola's garage. Look,"

Sheryl says, and she shows me a name embroidered on it: Ernie Bulosan. Lolo's. We run our fingers across the belt, and flashbacks of building with him spring into my head. "Wow. Thank you, Manang."

I snap it around my waist.

"Now, that's more like it," Alexa says.

I catch a glimpse in the full-length mirror. It goes with my shorts and plain tee, but if I were wearing a dress, it'd go with that, too. It feels just right.

Is this thirteen?

"Okay, final touch," Gracie says. She holds out a black blindfold, the velvety kind that people sleep in, and slides it down my head to cover my eyes. "Ta-da!"

It's a lot different from protective goggles.

"Where are we going?" I ask. "A fancy dinner and show downtown?"

"Exactly," Sheryl says. I can hear her smile.

Someone spins me and my head wobbles as I try to walk.

"What are you doing?"

"I don't know."

"Where are you taking me?"

"I don't know."

We're outside now; I feel the breeze on my legs and hear a car door opening. They push me inside like they're holding me for ransom. Someone tugs a seat belt over my shoulder and it clicks.

"Who's driving?" I ask.

"No one."

"Yep. This is one of those automatic cars."

The engine starts and music plays. All the way to wherever we're going the girls belt out pop tunes and blow at my face or stick their fingers in my ears. I have no idea how much time passes — because they're silly and singing as we feel the bump of car and road.

When the engine finally stops, they shout, "We're here, Birthday Girl!"

"Can you see anything?" Gracie's voice asks.

"Everything."

"Shut up," Sheryl says. "We're being

serious."

"Can I take the blindfold off now?"

"Quiet!" Alexa says like a sergeant.

"Shhhht! Shhhht!" Gracie says like a *lola* might, in her most exaggerated Filipino accent, and the girls bust up.

"Okay . . . now!" they say, and someone slips off the mask.

We're in Auntie's car, but with Mom in the driver's seat, grinning.

"Mom, you were in on this?"

"The whole time. Happy birthday, sweetie."

Finally, I can look out.

A group of people stand around my unfinished house laughing and talking, holding old-fashioned bottles of root beer. Streamers in pastel colors and paper lanterns hang from the trees, softly waving. It looks like a pretty postcard.

As soon as I step out they yell, "Surprise!"

I spot Jack holding up his camera. Mr. Keller and Ed, Annie, my cousins, lots of our family. Lola plants kisses on both of my cheeks and places a ring of flowers atop my head. "I made this from the wildflowers on your land."

I notice something new about my house: There's more to it now. Four wall frames stand vertically from the base of the trailer bed. They're not filled in, but it's a huge step.

Someone put a ton of effort into my house — but it wasn't me!

I walk up to it and place my hand on a beam to feel if it's real.

"Where did this framing come from?"

"We all helped," Sheryl says.

"We?" I say, so surprised.

"Yeah, a bunch of us," Gracie explains. "While you were at your class with Annie. Mr. Keller led us — it was your mom's idea. We had so much fun. Auntie Minda even brought lunch from In-N-Out."

"That was my favorite part," Arwin says, grinning.

"You know how you're always talking about how you like making things with your hands, Louie?" Alexa says. "It took us a while to figure out what that meant, but you were right. It feels good."

"I call it Habitat for Loumanity," Manang Maribel says, and we laugh.

Mr. Keller turns on his boom box and party music plays.

Mom takes my hand and walks me off to the side.

"I have your other gift."

"That class was expensive, Mom. You didn't have to get me anything else."

"No, this is a different kind of surprise." She smiles. "I've decided not to take the job out of state."

I gasp. "What? Are you kidding?"

Mom shakes her head and laughs. "Not joking. I'm going to accept the position in Oakland."

I'm in total shock. "What happened?"

"Your *lola*'s right — we shouldn't be away from our family. Look what they did for us. We're so lucky to have them." She beams at me. "It may mean we can't get our own place right away, but it's okay. I'm grateful for everything we have. And this job's not perfect, but I'll learn all I can and apply for better jobs later. I'll find what I need here. This will still open doors for us."

"Sooooo . . . we're staying put?" Mom nods. I grab her hands and jump all around. Laughter bubbles out of me. "Yeeeaaahh!" I shout.

"The tiny house is all yours," she says.

"You mean it's all *ours*." I do the happiest dance.

When Mom and I rejoin the party, Auntie Gemma points to the creek and says to me, "The kids went that way."

I run down the path and find my cousins and friends in the creek wading ankle-deep. "Hey!" I shout, waving my arms all around. "Guess what? We're not moving! We're staying!"

The girls scream and cheer and jump. "This calls for a water fight!" Sheryl yells, stomping water toward Arwin.

"Stop getting me wet!" he shouts, and that just makes them splash more water at him. Arwin sprints back toward the clearing and the other kids make their way up — except Jack and me.

"Hey," I say.

"Hey," he says.

I have a hard time looking Jack in the eye, even though we're friends now.

"Thank you for all the videos. . . . What they showed at the news studio, that was so awesome."

"Not bad, huh? I can put it on my demo reel now."

"You're really talented, you know?"

Now he's the one who has a hard time making eye contact.

"Should we go back up?" I ask.

"I have something for you first." From his pocket, Jack pulls out his phone.

"A new phone? Awww, you shouldn't have," I joke.

"Here," he says, swiping through before handing it to me.

"Is this your film-camp application?"

He shakes his head. "It's your birthday gift."

A video's on the screen, and I press Play.

The first person to pop up looks frazzled, but then the camera widens and you see why: She's working hard at making something. It's almost the same video that the station played, but there's a little more to it, with pictures of everyone important to me added at the very end.

Watching this video, I realize how many people have helped — especially Jack.

"Wow . . . this is so cool." Finally, I look at him and the butterflies tumble. "It's the best DIY project I've ever seen. Thanks so much. I love it."

"Sheryl gave me the pictures. I'll send you a copy."

I surprise myself by giving Jack a hug — an ultra-awkward tight squeeze around his neck. He smells like soap, the green bar kind.

"You're a good friend," I say.

Alexa thinks Jack should be my first kiss. If only I knew how that would happen.

But here's the magic thing: He comes in close and quick so that our faces touch this time, on the lips. I can't believe it. Tingles explode all over. Is this really happening? A true first kiss, clumsy and perfect and mine.

CHAPTER 26
WHEREVER I AM,
I'VE GOT SOME IDEAS

I stand on my bed in my new room, taping images onto a brand-new heart collage on the wall, one by one, like a puzzle.

"Pizza's here, break time! Come eat
now! Come eat!" Lola shouts from the
living room.

Moving day has turned into a party,
with uncles carrying in boxes, aunties in
the kitchen stocking cupboards, and
Mom excited and ready to decorate.

Mom's worked at her Oakland job for
seven months. We found a two-bedroom

close to Lola's and my cousins, and the rent's a good deal because Lola knew somebody who knew somebody.

It's not a tiny house, but it's pretty perfect. Because here's what I know: Home isn't necessarily a place; it's more of a feeling — of comfort and trust, of people who are a part of you. And I'm lucky, because it means I have a lot of different homes.

The house on my land has a foundation and walls filled in now. It still needs a roof and wiring, plumbing and floorboards, plus a lovely shade of paint. I'm thinking white with international orange on the door to make it pop. But I have time.

I'm not sure how long it will take to finish; I'm in the second semester of eighth grade, so I only have weekends. Sometimes Mom helps, or whoever wants to — usually somebody does. This house belongs to a lot of other people now. I just want to finish building it so everyone can come hang out.

In the meantime, there's school and working at the salvage yard, and friends, like Jack. We haven't shared any more kisses, but we still talk about everything. He even invited me to Spring Fling, and of course I said yes! Alexa's planning my outfit.

Mom likes her new job. Our money problems haven't disappeared, but I see how hard she works — the way my whole family does — and it makes me do the same. So I study hard. I started a blog and put up how-to videos, and I've gotten comments from tiny-house lovers all over the world who share their tips. We cheer each other on. Sure, I'm only thirteen, but my ideas matter.

There's one last gap in the middle of my heart collage. I slap a picture into the spot: me, staring off like an explorer. In the distance, the smallest house, holding the biggest love inside. The photo droops at one edge, so I smooth it down.

Lola has a favorite saying: *Home is where your heart is.* If that's true, then my home is wherever I am. And if people are houses, I'm a tiny one.

Sheryl runs in and leaps onto the bed. We tumble into a heap, busting up. "Pizza party!" She jumps to her feet.

"Be there in a sec," I say as she runs out.

I unpack the last box, the one with *Michael Nelson* scrawled on the side, holding all the videotapes. There's something else in there — a fallen piece of wood I found behind my house the other day. I started by sawing it, but like most beginnings, it's not much. No real shape, no nothing. Still, I've got some ideas.

I study the block in my hands. The sun shines in through the window, warming my new room, filling it.

My original idea was to make a keepsake holder, but now I'm not so sure. It's okay; I'm learning that sometimes plans change, so I guess I'll find out.

I turn and turn the wood.

I've already sanded it down to take off the rough edges. Parts of it are smooth; others are bumpy. Really, I'm just aiming for the start of something. Right now it feels good. It feels like possibilities.

ACKNOWLEDGMENTS

What makes a house a home? I've loved exploring this question. I've also loved sharing one snippet of Filipino American life through Lou's journey. Growing up, I never saw my family in the books I read (and I read a lot!), so giving my kids the chance to recognize aspects of their culture in an everyday story is something I'm very proud of.

I owe a world of gratitude to many people who've made this book possible:

I've had the best debut experience, thanks to the team at Wendy Lamb Books and Penguin Random House.

I'm grateful to work with my editor, Wendy Lamb, who helped me to dig deep and find the voice and heart of this book. I still can't believe how fortunate I've been to write my first novel with you;

I've learned so much, due to your thoughtfulness, patience, and expertise. Thank you for championing Lou's story.

A huge thank-you to Dana Carey, assistant editor, for your keen insight, enthusiasm, and care throughout this process.

To Sarah Davies, my amazing agent, thank you for being excited about this book from the start and for guiding me on the road to publication. Setting roots within Greenhouse Literary has been a dream come true.

A massive thanks to the following writer/editor friends, teachers, librarians, and historians for their helpful notes during various drafts: Cathy De Leon, Joanna Fabicon, Dawn Bohulano Mabalon, Alexia Paul, and Rachel Sarah. I also had two smart young readers who offered their thoughtful reactions: Koa De Leon and Eloise O'Day.

Much appreciation to Sandra Kacharos from the County of Marin and Cassie O'Mara of the Tumbleweed Tiny House Co. for answering my many research questions.

A special thanks to Hedgebrook for

providing me with a magical residency and the time, space, and nourishment to focus on revisions.

I'll always be grateful to the late Les Plesko and his workshops. A PEN Center USA Emerging Voices Fellowship set me off on the right path long ago and introduced me to my fellow "Pennies," who've given me loads of friendship, support, page-swaps, and writing dates through the years: Candice L. Davis, Natali Petricic Escobedo, Taylur Ngo, Melissa Roxas, and Eduardo Santiago.

I'm lucky for my wonderful parents, Restie and Tina, and for the Koerner, Medrano, and Respicio families (shout-out to all my awesome cousins!).

To my three most important people — Mark, Alden, and Cael — you inspire me every day . . . I love you! Thank you, Mark, for our stable, loving home, and the support to pursue my writing goals amid our ever-evolving family life.

And finally, a special thanks to you, the reader — I hope you enjoyed Lou's journey.

What kind of house are you?

ABOUT THE AUTHOR

Mae Respicio grew up in Northern California and has great memories of spending childhood summers dancing in a Filipino folk-dance troupe. Mae is a past recipient of a PEN Center USA Emerging Voices Fellowship. She's been a writer-in-residence at Hedgebrook and Atlantic Center for the Arts and has published a variety of musings on parenthood. She lives with her family in the San Francisco Bay Area, not far from the ocean and the redwoods. This is her first novel. Visit her at maerespicio.com.